# ONE ROTTEN APPLE AND OTHER STORIES

# ONE ROTTEN APPLE AND OTHER STORIES

Vandana Kumari Jena

olive turtle

NIYOGI BOOKS

Published by
**NIYOGI BOOKS**
Block D, Building No. 77,
Okhla Industrial Area, Phase-I,
New Delhi-110 020, INDIA
Tel: 91-11-26816301, 26818960
Email: niyogibooks@gmail.com
Website: www.niyogibooksindia.com



Editor: Saachi Khurana
Design: Shraboni Roy

ISBN: 978-93-86906-17-5
Publication: 2018



Printed at: Niyogi Offset Pvt. Ltd., New Delhi, India

To Prasanna, my companion of 35 years,
who now lives on in my memories.

# Contents

# Blood Lies

There is something oppressive about silence. Everyone is afraid to break it. I can see the fear mirrored on the faces of the people surrounding me. Papa has it lurking in his eyes. The sight of a uniformed officer in our home does not bode well. Having been the father of a police officer for years, he knows all too well what it means. Mummy decides to sit down on a chair and rock herself rhythmically. The rocking seems to calm her. Barun pulls his lower lip down and runs his tongue over it nervously. He reminds me of a lizard with its tongue darting in and out. Aarti, our maid, turns her back to the officer and looks into the garden. I wonder if she is really able to enjoy the profusion of flowers or if this is her means of escape. Raghav remains frozen, as though someone had shouted "statue" and forgotten to say "over." There is only one way to break this silence. I speak.

"What brings you here, officer?" I ask. There is a palpable sense of relief in the room. Faces that earlier seemed to have frozen in a tableau now begin to get animated. The officer moves forward and almost holds my hand in his. I eye his large hand with its black hair warily. He drops it by his side almost immediately. He then begins to grope for words.

"Ma'am," he says and then falls silent again. Whatever he has to say is difficult to utter. He is unable to find the right words. Somehow, I suspect that he had practiced his little speech on the way to our house but had hoped to encounter just one or two persons. Maybe it is the crowd in the drawing room that intimidates him, or perhaps he is afraid of me.

It was not he but someone else who had come a month ago to break the shattering news of Abhi's demise. The man had no realisation that he had walked into a party; it was Barun's 17th birthday. I had seen the shock on the officer's face when he entered, just as Barun blew out the birthday candles and we all began singing, "Happy birthday to you." There was mourning writ large upon the officer's face and he could obviously not school his expression into one of happiness. "It's Abhi, isn't it?" I had asked. "I am so sorry, Ma'am," he had muttered. "Abhijeet Sinha's apartment in Kosovo was bombed this afternoon."

Kosovo. The image of the city flashed before my eyes. We had been to Kosovo almost two years ago. Barun had been coached by Abhi during his summer vacation for his class X examinations. I closed my eyes and visualised Abhi's apartment building. It was brownish black and dilapidated from the outside but surprisingly well-furnished inside. An old-fashioned lift took one to the fourth floor, unless of course one preferred to take the steep and at times uneven stone stairs. A small pizza parlour at the ground floor ensured that there was always a throng of customers outside the apartment building.

We all knew that Kosovo was dangerous. While taking us through the mountains, Abhijeet had shown us the red flags that had indicated the presence of landmines; even so, nothing had prepared me for this.

"They bombed his apartment," the officer repeated. "He must have died instantaneously."

Both he and I knew that this was not true. Abhi must have burnt to death slowly. He must have felt his hair singe and flesh burn. He must have smelt the acrid stench of burning flesh as he perished. He must have died agonisingly. By the time the fire brigade came, he must have been dead.

"Death need not have been so painful," I had said, after an interminable silence. Barun had asked me for an unforgettable party for his 17th birthday. He had got his wish. I was reminded of the short story, 'The Monkey's Paw' and the unexpected way in which the family's wish for money was fulfilled, by way of compensation for the death of their only son. The party was over. The guests, mostly Barun's classmates, disappeared soon after the officer left.

What now? I wonder. What could it be this time? What could be worse than Abhi's death?

"I don't know how to say it," says the officer, his face downcast, his eyes focused on a small black stain on the floor.

"There is only one way of saying it," I murmur. He looks at me expectantly and I say, "Just speak."

Somehow he lacks the courage to go on. Instead, he puts his hand into his pocket, takes out a wallet and fishes out a photograph. I see a petite woman with black hair and black eyes standing beside Abhi.

"What does it mean?" asks Papa in an unnaturally loud voice. "We are not here to play dumb charades."

The man gulps and mutters, "She claims to be his wife."

"What?" Papa's voice resounds in the drawing room, even as he brings his fist down on the glass tabletop. The ashtray jumps into the air and then topples onto the carpet, and the pile of coasters collapses on the floor like a pack of cards.

"She claims that she was married to him," the officer says hesitantly.

"That's nonsense," denies Papa. "My Abhi was not like that."

"She says she has proof of the wedding," says the officer.

"What is she?" I ask. "Serb or Albanian?"

"Albanian," he says.

"Mother Teresa was also Albanian," chimes in Barun. "Of Albanian descent," he corrects himself hastily as I glare at him. I wonder why I asked the question. Does it matter?

"It doesn't matter," I say briskly, "even if she claims that Abhi married her. In our country, bigamy is a crime. The second wife has no status; she has no rights."

The officer looks at me in amazement. I have taken the idea of Abhi's second wife in my stride. But with Abhi dead, how does it matter?

"But the child from a second marriage has rights," he argues in a low voice, "and the woman claims that she is carrying Abhi's child. The baby is expected any day now."

Papa's face begins to turn red. I see the veins sticking out in his forehead and I begin to get alarmed. Shocks are not good for his health and he has had one last month, when he lost Abhi. Papa hollers, "Tell the woman not to besmirch the memory of my only son; my son was a hero, not a villain."

"Abhi would never do something like that," says Raghav. I look at him in surprise, wondering if he always sounded so sanctimonious. I do not recall; I am seeing him after 15 years. He is only visiting to condole with us for Abhi's death.

"We could always run a DNA test, couldn't we?" asks Barun brashly. He watches too many movies and reads too much science fiction, except that DNA testing is science fiction no more. It is a reality.

"There is nothing of Abhi left here," I say flatly. The officer looks at me in surprise. "He took away everything with him to

Kosovo," I add. The police officer continues to look perplexed. "Abhi was posted in Kashmir," I explain, "and from there he left for Kosovo directly. He was there for five years. We shifted to this house only three months ago. Abhi has never been here."

The officer looks crestfallen. The DNA test would have solved his dilemma. I can understand his compulsions. Abhi had not merely earned a UN pension but had also been covered for an insurance of one million dollars. A DNA test would prove whether the Albanian woman carries his child or not.

"Is there nothing, nothing at all of Abhijeet Sinha?" the officer asks.

"Officer, his clothes, his belongings, his books were all in Kosovo," I murmur. "He was paid to get them shipped there."

"Is there nothing that is his?" he asks once again.

"There is," I say, and all eyes in the room are riveted towards me. "There is Barun." He looks at me wonderingly. "Can't the doctors test the DNA of both children to find out if they had the same father?" I ask. I see a look of admiration in his eyes. He probably wonders if I am willing to share Abhijeet with another woman, in case the DNA turns out to be positive.

Papa is happy. He would do anything to save his son's memory from being sullied. Abhijeet's friend, Raghav, thinks I am being a fool. "Why invite trouble?" he asks me afterwards.

Three months later we have all but forgotten the visit of the police officer. Barun is sitting at the dining table, his hand inside a large bag of Ruffle's plain salted chips, while he pores over his books. I see him masticating, his jaws moving slowly as he crunches a mouthful of chips. He reminds me of Bruno, our black Labrador, who is salivating at the sight of the chicken drumstick Aarti had offered him. Barun wants to be an engineer. It is what his father wanted. It becomes so important to fulfil a dying man's wish. Barun has decided to sacrifice his dream of being a bass guitarist to be an engineer. Perhaps Abhi's soul will now rest in peace.

When the doorbell rings Aarti goes to open the door. The police officer Aditya Virmani is at the doorstep. There is a half-guilty look on his face. What is it?

"Sit down," I say to him graciously. After all, this is his second visit to our home and that makes him an acquaintance of sorts.

"There is a test," he says, his words coming out in a rush, as though he has a well-rehearsed script but is afraid that there will be no one to prompt him if he misses his cue. "It is called the Y-STR Male Lineage test."

Barun looks up from his textbook and listens intently. He thrives on trivia. Mr Virmani continues, "The Y-STR male lineage test is used to determine whether two or more males are related through their paternal lineage."

I look at Mr Virmani in admiration. Is he a Biology major or has he merely mugged up passages from the internet?

"This test focuses on the Y chromosome and results in a unique Y-STR profile for each male who is tested. If a male child and his alleged half-brother want to know if they have the same biological father, and it turns out that they have the same Y-STR profile, it is practically proven that they share the same father. If the profiles do not match..." At this point, the officer's voice peters out as he shrugs his shoulders expressively. Without saying anything else, he has disclosed one thing. The Albanian woman has given birth to a son.

"How long would it take the results to show up?" I ask.

"Just five days," he says, beaming.

"But the Albanian woman's son is in Kosovo."

He begins to look sheepish. I notice the half-guilty look on his face once again. I cannot make out what it means. "Does he plan to take Barun to Kosovo?" I say to myself. I will not allow it.

The officer looks at me imploringly, walks out of the house and walks in with a petite Albanian woman who has a baby nestled in her arms. She is very beautiful. But that does not surprise me. Most of the women I saw in Kosovo were beautiful. There is an air of vulnerability about her that Abhi must have found appealing. No wonder he fell in love with her. But her shoulders are hunched and her eyes are sad. Perhaps she did love Abhi and is still grieving his loss.

"Get out; tell her to get out," shouts Papa, and the woman, who looks like a half-woman, half-child, cowers in fear and rushes out of the house. Papa has made his antipathy to her evident. I look around to gauge the reaction of the others in the room. Barun looks awestruck. Mummy's face is inscrutable. I have no idea what she is thinking. Does she want this child to be her grandson? Does she want Abhi's genes to live on, in not just Barun but this child as well? I will never know. Aarti, however, cannot disguise her surprise. Like Barun, she is struck by the woman's beauty. She cannot blame Abhi for straying.

"The test will be done in India. Shahin has insisted on coming here for the test," says Aditya Virmani.

Barun mutters, "She doesn't trust us." He loves to state the obvious.

"How long will it take for the results to come out?" I say once again.

"Five days," confirms the officer.

"I am ready whenever you are," says Barun, although no one asked him for his opinion. He shoves his hand into his bag of chips and begins chomping again.

Aditya Virmani takes Barun to the All India Institute of Medical Sciences the next day and I decide to accompany him. Like Shahin, I am concerned that the tests should not be messed up.

The next five days are the most difficult ones of our lives. As usual, we pretend that everything is normal. Mummy spends more time in the prayer room. Papa buries his face in the newspaper while I watch the television, switching channels with great adroitness, my attention span not exceeding five minutes on shows that I used to be glued onto in the past. On the sixth day, we are all tense. Papa paces around the drawing room like a caged lion. Mummy sits and rocks her chair as if her very life depends on it. Barun puts the stopwatch in action and begins to attempt the IIT JEE mock question paper as though it is the real thing. I sit with a novel in my hand, my eyes glued on to the door, waiting for the bell to ring.

At last, it does. Aditya Virmani enters with a big smile on his face. "The tests prove conclusively that the two children are not related; they cannot have the same father," he beams.

"Does that woman know?" I ask, not willing to utter her name.

"She does," he discloses.

"And what does she say?" I cannot resist asking him.

"She says something is terribly wrong. She swears by the Lord that her child is Abhijeet Sinha's son," he mutters. "She says one day she will prove it."

"Science can never be wrong," states Barun solemnly, as if he is the Oracle of Delphi.

"The slut," says Papa softly, but the venom with which he says it makes me cringe.

"Something is terribly wrong," Shahin had said, and she was right. Something was very wrong indeed. Only I know the truth. Only I know of the truth that drove Abhi from me and kept him away for the last many years. Only I know the suspicion he had and the courage he lacked, in asking me to undergo this Agnipariksha, the DNA test to prove that Barun was his son. He suspected, but could never confirm, that while he was away in Kashmir some 18 years ago, I was guilty of adultery. Barun is not Abhi's son. Barun is Raghav's son. I knew the outcome of the test before it was undertaken.

"There is something terribly wrong," Shahin had said, "and one day I will prove it."

I can understand her dismay. If the DNA test had turned out to be positive, her son would have been entitled to a share in Abhi's wealth. But it is not about money alone; it is her reputation that is at stake. Besides, she wants her son to share his father's name. I am afraid of her threats. Today, traces of a man's DNA can be found in many of his possessions. I hope Shahin has none of Abhi's.

Aditya Virmani told me that Abhi's marriage had been kept a secret. According to Shahin, Abhi could never meet her in her house. It was she who visited him at his home. And Abhi's home had been destroyed by a bomb. Everything of his had turned into ashes.

I must begin destroying anything and everything that has association with Abhi. And now I have an excuse for it. I am the distraught wife of a dead man, who, a woman half my age claims, was married to her as well. In a way I am glad that we are Hindus, and that Abhi's ashes, having been scattered in the Ganges, are at one with the elements. I do not really think that she will be able to prove anything. I look at Barun and smile.

# Initiation Rites

A moment can change one's life. Mine changed when I boarded the train at Raigarh station, just as it began to leave the platform. I began to run when the guard blew his whistle, my feet flying on the concrete. I made it to the AC II tier compartment just as the train gathered speed, adrenalin pumping hard, beads of perspiration on my forehead, a veritable Jesse Owen after his Olympic sprint. It took an enormous effort for me to pull my black strolley bag onto the footboard, and as I took in large gulps of air, helping hands ushered me inside.

As I walked towards my berth, my head discreetly bent, I saw a man, his head bowed, backpack on his shoulders, walking away. "Misogynist, he got up and left the moment he saw you coming," murmured the man sitting on the side bunk. I slid towards my berth and shoved my bag under it when I heard a voice say, "That was dangerous, jumping onto a moving train. You might have been killed."

My head jerked up immediately, like a marionette on a string. The man on the upper berth across my seat, whom I had not noticed so far, had made the pronouncement. He was elderly. His hair had turned almost white. But his face seemed smooth and unlined. Was he 60 or 80? I had no idea. He looked avuncular. Immediately I labelled him Grandpa.

"I got late," I mumbled, wondering if this would turn out to be an interrogation.

"But I thought I saw you standing at the bookshop on the platform," another voice intruded on the conversation. I looked up in surprise at a bearded man of an indeterminate age, sitting on the opposite berth, who reminded me in a strange way of Fidel Castro. He was short and stocky and looked tough and a little ruthless. I nicknamed this one The Rebel. "I was undecided about boarding the train," I admitted. "I could not make up my mind till the very end, when the train was about to leave."

"Running away from home."

I turned towards the man sitting by my side, who had spoken. He was young and very good looking. Barely 30, I surmised.

"Yash," he winked conspiratorially at me as he handed me his business card. "Yash Chibber, assistant manager, Airtel."

I felt my cheeks burn slowly. He did not know how close to home his remark had been.

The arrival of the waiter made for a welcome break. "One vegetarian lunch," I ordered, realising that I had had nothing since morning except a black coffee and a toast. The man dumped an aluminium-foil-covered tray before me. Even the watery *arhar* dal, unappetising potato and peas curry, chapattis, and cold rice did not deter me from eating hungrily.

"Definitely running away from home," chuckled Yash as he saw me wolfing down my lunch. My eyes widened in dismay. "Otherwise you would have received a send-off from your family—father, mother, brother, sister, nephew or niece," asserted Yash. "Along with containers of home-cooked food, pulao, puris, chicken, bhindi, and home-made *aam ka achar*. You would not be eating this muck," he added.

I lowered my head so that he would not see the colour drain away from my face. Home. When had I left home? Today?

Yesterday? Or was it months ago? I had lost track of time. My presence within the four walls of my house had not mattered. My heart had been far away.

"Running away from home to marry someone against your family's wishes," hazarded Yash, who revelled in his role of a self-appointed sleuth, "someone from a different religion, caste or region."

He was surprisingly perceptive. Yes, there was someone. Someone who was different from anyone I had ever known. Charismatic, passionate, and fiery. An iconoclast, a revolutionary, an enigma. A passionate ideologue and a recluse. Someone before whom nothing mattered to me—no right or wrong, no family or friends, nothing. Someone for whom I was willing to walk to the end of the earth.

I remembered the first time I saw Aftab. It was at the university; he was giving a fiery speech, contesting for the post of Students' Union President. His impassioned speech left me spellbound. He was a visionary. Someone who could ignite dreams, kindle passions and make his utopia seem possible. Hearing his voice, I could feel goosebumps on my arms. But I knew that I was one among a thousand girls who were stirred by his words. For a moment I thought I saw his eyes rest on me. And then I saw him smile. Perhaps it was only my imagination, or perhaps it was wishful thinking. I was a part of the crowd. While he, as a potential president of the Students' Union, stood apart.

A few days later, I met Aftab in a jam-packed bus. I was certain he would not recognise me. But he put a hand on my shoulder and as I shook under his touch he grinned. "Vote for me," he urged.

He need not have asked. I would have died for him.

"I know you will," he said knowingly. "I saw you in my rally."

I was perplexed. How could he notice me in such a large crowd? Then I remembered that his eyes had rested on me fleetingly that day and he had smiled. I thought my heart would burst. Maybe my destiny was calling me. I threw caution to the winds and revelled in the fact that he had sought me out.

That accidental meeting had led to many more, and I reeled under the impact of his eyes on mine, the touch of his skin on mine, the male tangy freshness of his breath, the passion in his voice, his ardent possession and my willing surrender. Our lives began to blend inextricably and I knew I could never separate mine from his.

I was grateful for the sudden silence that fell in the compartment. I looked furtively at the man on the side berth. But for his first remark he had remained silent all throughout. Through the window I saw green fields, with some unknown crop, fluttering in the wind. A dog raced against the train for some time and then gave up. A shabby scarecrow, clad in an old tweed coat, striped pants and a straw hat, stood sentinel in the rice field. Five children, three boys and two girls, held hands and encircled the scarecrow. A brightly coloured kite soared across the sky. Someone was celebrating his happiness by this burst of activity. A village woman in a yellow saree was bringing food for the farmer who was struggling to plough the earth. A pair of oxen drooped in the heat.

For the next five or ten minutes the five of us sat in companionable silence. "I hope someone is meeting you in Delhi," Grandpa's voice intruded into my thoughts. I nodded my head. I knew Aftab would be there for me when I arrived in Delhi.

"Why?" It was the Rebel who asked.

"It's 14th August today," said Uncle. "There is Red Alert in and around Delhi. You must avoid going to public places; there is a danger of bomb blasts."

I shivered at the thought.

"Have you been to Delhi before?" he asked me, almost as an afterthought.

"Yes," I mumbled, and then seeing the questioning look on his face, I added, "I once came to Delhi as an NCC Cadet for the Republic Day Parade."

"You?" exclaimed Yash incredulously, boldly appraising my diminutive frame. "Someone as petite as you was an NCC Cadet?"

"She is planning her own Independence Day," remarked the taciturn gentleman on the side berth, "or maybe she is trading her independence for the shackles of marriage!"

"15 August 1947. India attained its Independence that year; I was a young man then," ruminated Grandpa, "and I was a freedom fighter. I had taken part in the Quit India Movement."

His eyes shone with pride. I closed my eyes and sepia images of the freedom struggle floated in my mind. Images of Gandhiji, of helmeted British policemen raining blows on hapless Satyagrahis, including Grandpa. Images I had seen in history textbooks and while watching Films Division documentaries in the cinema halls. What would be Grandpa's age, I wondered. Not a day less than 85, I was certain. Had he been to prison? If yes, then for how long? Was he disillusioned by the world today? Had he been a little like Aftab in his youth?

"I was a follower of Jai Prakash Narain," murmured the Rebel, his voice tinged with regret. "I took part in his Total Revolution Movement in 1974. We wasted two years of our lives for the movement." His eyes had a faraway look in them.

I was surprised by his revelation. I would not have guessed that he had been an idealist, although today he was clearly disillusioned. But appearances were obviously deceptive.

"I was a Naxal sympathiser," quipped the man on the side berth. Suddenly all eyes were riveted towards him. He was clearly enjoying this unexpected attention. He saw the look of scepticism in my gaze. Lifting his leg, he pushed his right trouser up to his knee. "I have a wooden leg," he murmured. "I lost it in a police firing."

"Naxal sympathiser, police firing, wooden leg, Independence day, Red alert." The words began popping up in my mind at frequent intervals. Suddenly my insides began to churn. I felt bile rise in my mouth and panicked. Edging my way past the men who were lounging nearby, I rushed towards the two bathrooms, but they were closed. I then headed towards the washbasin located outside the bathroom and, retching loudly, threw up into it. As the rancid smell of vomited food began to suffuse the corridor, the men hanging by the door moved towards their seats. I opened my purse and searched through its contents.

A bathroom door opened just then. And there he was, minus his backpack.

"Quick," said Aftab, as he opened the door of the train. The sudden blast of air took me by surprise. I clutched the door handle and stood quivering, unable to take the final plunge towards the fields. We were whizzing past the countryside and I looked with terror as the train passed a lamp post and then moved towards the bridge.

"Quick," he said once again, and when he saw me paralysed with fear, he snatched my purse and pushed me out, before pressing the detonator and jumping after me. I hit the ground hard and rolled over the mud before I came to a stop.

The blast occurred just as the train entered the bridge. The intensity of it was enormous. The old bridge bent and there was a tearing sound as the steel girders snapped before the bridge was breached. A bogie hung precariously on the edge of the bridge before plunging straight into the river. My black strolley bag had exploded. A minute later there was another blast. This time I knew it was Aftab's backpack.

I heard the sounds of the screams resonating in the air, followed by the splintering of glass. The compartments were enveloped in a cloud of black smoke as angry orange flames licked the train. I imagined the faces of the passengers filled with fear, the sheer panic on the faces of men, women and children as realisation dawned upon them that bombs had been detonated. I imagined the smell of scorching flesh and the blood, gore and mayhem that followed, with men and women dying, and children burnt to cinders. I knew that the RDX and aluminium nitrate that had been used in the bombs would have wrenched arms and legs from torsos, shredded human flesh, killed some and maimed many. And those who survived the blast would have been sucked into the vortex of the swirling waters below.

It was terrifying. But even more terrifying was the satisfaction on Aftab's expression as he said, "Mission accomplished." I trembled on seeing his face. "Stop shivering," he commanded.

"They must all be dead," I whispered. "Grandpa, Yash, everyone. There must be families waiting for them at home who would never see them again because of me."

"Pray that they are dead, and that there are no eyewitnesses left; otherwise they will be able to identify you," retorted Aftab.

I thought of Grandpa, who thought I was vulnerable and had advised me to be careful, as Delhi was on Red Alert. If only he knew the truth, I thought hysterically. No one would have guessed my mission and understood my reluctance to board the train.

But I had chosen a life with Aftab. For me, these were initiation rites. But I still could not contain the look of horror on my face as I saw bogies after bogies plunging into the river. Long after the bombs had exploded I could still hear the cries of terror. I put my hands on my ears to blot out the sound. Aftab put his arms around me and said, "Hush, forget it. It's over."

But I knew he was wrong. It was not over. There would be many new missions we would have to accomplish.

# The Choice

*The Los Angeles Times*, dated 3 September 2004, lies open on the dining table. My eyes are riveted on the news item by Kim Murphy, "When a mother was made to choose between her two children." I read the news slowly.

> In Beslan, Russia, Zalina Dzandarova cradled her son Alan as he slept with his small face buried against her stomach. He was the child that Dzandarova was able to save, the child she chose to save, really. It was the other one, little Alana, her six-year-old daughter, whose image tormented her: Alana clutching her hand, Alana crying and calling after her. Alana's sobs disappearing into the distance as Dzandarova rushed out of Middle School No. 1 here on Thursday, clutching Alan in her arms. Guerrillas armed with automatic rifles and explosive belts allowed 26 women and children to leave. About a dozen mothers, like Dzandarova, were allowed to take only one child and forced to leave another behind.

Ma is sitting on the chair by my side, her eyes on me. As I finish reading the newspaper and keep it aside, she reaches for it. She reads the newspaper, oblivious to the world, heedless of the fact that her tea is growing cold and that a fly has begun to hover dangerously close to her half-eaten egg.

"Terrible, isn't it?" clucks Aunt Saras in sympathy. "It is a choice no woman should have to make."

A gentle shudder passes through Ma's slender fame. "No," she says, in a voice so low that I can barely catch the words.

"She chose the boy, didn't she?" asks Rati, and her mother looks at her indignantly.

"She chose the younger child," Aunt Saras rebukes her, "He just happened to be a boy; she had no choice really."

"We are all," says Rati,"in the grip of terrorism."

"9/11 has changed the entire world. It has made the word 'trust' disappear from our lexicon. It has made us realise how vulnerable we all are," says Aunt Saras.

But Ma and I barely hear their words. Her eyes lock onto mine and then I look away. I cannot bear to see them so tortured and pained. Both she and I know what she is thinking. 9/11 was not the beginning. I am thinking of that terrible day some eight years ago that changed our lives irrevocably.

It was a sleepy summer afternoon in Manipur, a troubled, insurgency-prone, hilly state in north-eastern India. The air was suffused with the smell of roses, the humming of honey bees, and the occasional growl of a dog. Both Mani, my younger brother, and I, were asleep, when Ma woke us up.

"Get up," she said, "we have to attend a function."

Mani started crying. Ma immediately put him in her lap, although he was now more than two years old. "Come, Charu, get up," she said, shaking me by the shoulder. "Get dressed."

That is why we were dressed at 3.30 pm that Saturday afternoon, to be present at the parade ground in the district headquarters at Thoubal by 4 pm.

Papa was away on training, but Ma insisted that Papa would have wanted us to represent him at the official function. The parade ground was packed. The entire town seemed to have congregated there, although I now know that it could accommodate only a thousand persons at best. Ma held Mani in her arms and clutched my hand. She was ushered in and taken to the second row, just behind the VIP seats. She smiled with pleasure, for Papa was just a middle-rung officer in the Central Reserve Police Force. Mani put his thumb into his mouth and Ma tried in vain to pull it out. His lower lip began to protrude. The chief guest arrived just then and we stood up as the flag was unfurled.

When the crackling sound was first heard no one quite understood what it was. Firecrackers? They were supposed to be lit at the end of the function, as a part of the grand finale. Why was the crackle, the sizzle and the smoke coming now, when the programme had just begun? The next time the crackling sounds erupted we realised what they were.

Gunfire.

Suddenly light-skinned men in Khaki uniforms with masks over their faces barged onto the ground. With guns in their hands and eyes full of hatred, they were men who wanted to wreak revenge upon the Central Reserve Police Force for swooping down upon them in their hideout and killing their comrades a few days before.

I saw Ma's face, with her mouth wide open. The babble of voices was replaced by total silence. Everyone was petrified. Then I heard Mani raise his voice and bawl. His voice, never feeble, had now reached a crescendo. Ma tried to put a hand on his mouth but he dug his teeth into her soft flesh until she yelped with pain. An armed insurgent came and plucked him from her hands and slapped him on the cheek, and deposited him back in Ma's arms. Mani howled even louder. All heads turned towards Ma. Her face turned ashen.

"Tell him to shut up," hissed the insurgent.

"Get out, get out; leave immediately," shouted their commander, who was standing on the dais, his gun trained on the chief guest.

Ma looked uncertainly in my direction.

"Leave right now," he bellowed, "or I will kill you and that brat."

The armed insurgent next to her prodded her with his gun, again and again. "Leave," he growled. "Take that brat and leave immediately."

"Ma," I called out, my voice hoarse with fear. "Ma," I cried once again, trying to clutch her saree.

Ma shivered, looked at the guard scowling at her, then at the commander on the dais, and saw them shake their heads imperceptibly. Then she put her hand on Mani's mouth, silencing his screams, and, pulling the saree from my hand, she walked away.

As she left, the commander at the dais shouted, "Everyone on their knees. Lie flat with your heads down. Don't move."

I saw everyone do as he said, their noses touching the gravel. But I was shell-shocked. Completely bewildered, I remained standing. Then the man next to me pushed me down. At the gate, when Ma turned back, she saw him bending over me, his body covering mine. For a moment she froze, her mouth open. Then slowly she dragged herself from the parade ground, where she knew mayhem would follow.

I have no idea what happened in the intervening hour. I could smell the sweat on the man's body, mingled with a strange musky scent. I felt his breath fan my face and I was reminded of the smell of disinfectants in the hospital. It was Sekmai, I learnt later, the famous alcohol made from fermented rice.

I looked into his eyes, small, brown and almost expressionless. Tiny red veins threaded the whites. His proximity did not disturb me. I did not understand its implication, or the implicit danger. I was but eight years old. I was not crushed by his weight; he rested most of it on his elbows. Then we heard some more shots. I saw the terror I felt within me mirrored in his eyes. Almost savagely, he raised his hand and turned me on my stomach. I felt the gravel rub against my nose, my cheeks and my chin. I closed my eyes.

Gunfire crackled once again. Bullets were sprayed all around. They fell here, there, everywhere. There was something familiar about the man whose body covered mine. I frowned, trying to remember if I had seen him before. Gunfire crackled once more. I wanted to cover my ears with my hands, for the noise seemed deafening.

However, the commander had said, "Don't move." No one moved. Suddenly, the man fell on top of me. I was almost crushed under his weight. But I still did not move, not until I heard the siren, the sounds of scuffle and the shouts, and finally the announcement in English and Manipuri saying that it was over. I crawled from under his body, rolled it away from mine, saw his glazed eyes, the gaping hole in his back, his blood-splattered shirt, and knew that he was dead.

For a long time, I stood there looking at the bodies of officers being taken away by the jawans, at the bodies scattered in the field, at the children screaming and the people crying. I crossed the parade ground, which was just a 15-minute walk from my house. The road was familiar to me as the parade ground was on the way to my school. I reached home grimy, with scratched knees and grazed elbows.

Ma was standing by the door, staring glassily at the gate, with Mani in her arms. I saw the look of terror in her eyes when she saw me return with grazed knees and elbows and blood splattered all over my frock.

"Are you alright, Charu?" she asked. "Did anything happen to you?" She looked at the blobs of blood all over my frock once again, and asked in a strange voice, "Charu, are you hurt?"

I thought of the ground I had just left. Littered on the earth were men who were dead, women who were dying and children who were bleeding. Lying on the ground was the man whose mouth reeked of Sekmai, who was now quite dead. Was I hurt? Indeed I was, but mine was not a physical hurt. I didn't say anything.

"Charu, are you hurt?" she began saying once again, but then she saw my set mouth and bleak eyes and kept quiet. The maid came and took me to the bathroom, helped me change my frock, cleaned my grazed knees and elbows with antiseptic and later on put me to sleep. I thought once again of the man who had rolled on top of me, dead, quite dead, and realised that, if he had not shielded me, I might have died instead.

No newspaper covered our story. There were more than 800 people who had gathered in the parade ground, and 28 among them were dead. Eight of them were officers. One of them was the chief guest. It was the dead and the dying who made news. No newspaper was interested to know about a mother and son who got away and a daughter who got left behind.

I have no idea what Ma told Papa on his return. But if he found me quiet and withdrawn afterwards he understood. "She has seen death at close quarters," he said. "No one can remain untouched by it. No wonder she has become withdrawn." He knew that this explained my silence, my occasional bouts of bad temper, and my recurrent nightmares.

"Charu?" Many a time I heard the pleading note in Ma's voice, but she could never ask me what happened that day. At that time, I did not understand the reason for her anxiety. All I could remember, whenever I looked at her, was her walking away with Mani and brushing away the hand of the daughter she was leaving behind. It was later, as an adolescent, that I understood the source of her worry, but I did nothing to alleviate it.

For eight long years she had suffered. For eight long years I had never forgiven her. But now, reading the newspaper, I wondered if she really had no choice. Would every other woman in her place have done the same? I am not quite sure.

Ma's eyes are resting on me and I see in them the question she had asked that summer, years ago. "I'm alright, Ma," I say. "I wasn't hurt."

Ma understands immediately. I see tension being slowly released from her face. She still has an unspoken question in her eyes. I know what it is. I will tell her later about my blood-splattered dress. I will tell her of the unknown man who had saved my life by shielding my body with his, of the bullet that had torn into his back, of his blood, which had splattered on my clothes. Why did he save my life? I will never know. Was he someone we knew? I cannot remember. Did he have a daughter at home? Did I remind him of her? I will never know.

One day I shall find out about the people who died that day and find out who he was. One day I shall meet his family and tell them that he was a hero. I look at the newspaper lying on the dining table and then at Ma, who had left her daughter behind at the parade ground. This daughter has come home at last.

# The Saviour

It was a day like no other, but Kabir did not know it yet. The street was busy, as it usually was on Friday afternoons. He walked slowly on the asphalt, his forehead puckered in a frown that was beginning to line his eyebrows, his lips pursed, the memories of the last half hour chasing him, mocking his presumptuousness and celebrating his disappointment.

Half an hour ago, hope had begun to die, but the shock had yet to set in. He did what he was good at, clearing his mind of all thoughts, making it as clean as a slate, trying to achieve a state of thoughtlessness, a nirvana of sorts. For him the street became a combat zone and he negotiated it accordingly. Involuntarily his lips began to curve into a smile. The bull staring at him, his horns jutting aggressively, was nothing less than a suspected landmine, as was the rickshaw that turned from a by-lane, sped before him, and jerked to a halt, making its lone passenger stagger and slip towards the floor of the rickshaw. It was only Kabir's dexterity and presence of mind that made him extend a helping hand to the passenger and prevented her from skidding onto the ground. A dhoti-clad man in a spotless white shirt spat out the remnants of a betel nut on the sidewalk, the crimson splattering and missing a pedestrian by inches. Kabir's steps took on a note of urgency as he moved ahead towards a sweet shop, where large *khoya* ladoos were being made as prasad for the nearby

Laxmi Narayan temple. The air was redolent with the smell of browning. He stood transfixed, watching the speed with which the *halwai* stirred it into a smooth paste.

Walking ahead, Kabir almost missed seeing the butcher's boy on his cycle. Carrying a large leg of mutton, the boy was riding hurriedly, perhaps thinking of an irate customer awaiting his order and an equally irate employer awaiting his return.

Crowds jostled with each other and Kabir smiled as he thought he heard the muezzin. There must be a mosque nearby, he thought to himself, but he had no idea where exactly. He had seldom come to this part of the town, and today he had found himself here simply because he wanted to get away from his own thoughts and become a part of the crowd. Suddenly, the bull he had left behind a little while ago began to rush down the street. Kabir stood at the kerb, leaning against the wall of a house in the narrow street. As the bull charged forward, it jostled the butcher's boy, who fell from the bicycle; the mutton leg went flying from his hand, landing in the large black container where the *khoya* was being cooked.

The butcher's boy whimpered, unable to get up. Someone extended his hand and pulled him to his feet. Kabir tore himself from the wall he was leaning against and walked ahead, muttering, "What happened?" as he saw a motley group of people rush towards the butcher's boy, whose topi had fallen down and was being trampled underfoot, His eyes were filled with dread at the prospect of being lynched by a mob.

The *namaaz* would be over soon, reckoned Kabir, and it was possible that after offering their prayers the men would come down this same street and a small incident would spark a conflagration. Communal violence, hitherto little known in this town, would be fanned and result in a full-blown communal riot. He glanced at the butcher's boy. Barely 16 years old, and looking strangely vulnerable without his topi on his head, he was begging the passers-by and saying, *"Yeh ek hadsa tha." It was an accident.*

Kabir saw a boy pick up a jagged stone, aim it straight at the butcher's boy, and fling it with full strength. As the stone found its mark and blood came out in spurts from the victim's forehead, the boy mimicked, *"Yeh ek hadsa tha."* The young Muslim boy stared at the crowd imploringly.

Everyone remained silent. Kabir knew that old memories were being rustled up in their minds. He could imagine men, old and bent, standing on the narrow balconies above the tiny shops, remembering the exodus during the Partition, their eyes dry as they remembered the womenfolk, mothers, wives, sisters and daughters they had lost during the partition because of loot, plunder, rape and death. He could see among the crowds men and women who had grown up hearing stories of the Partition and of what the families had lost—fields, houses, life and property—when they had crossed the border while leaving Pakistan and coming to India.

He was sure others were remembering it, too. He knew that for them this was payback time. People who had lived in harmony till they had been told they were two nations, not one, were now clearly divided. And the reason was that a piece of mutton had fallen into a utensil where *khoya* was being roasted to make ladoos.

Blood flowed from the butcher's boy's head and yet people were afraid to come to his rescue. Kabir was afraid that the crowd, growing restive by the minute, would lynch him. Suddenly he could not bear it any more. The butcher's boy could be his own younger brother. He could not desert him and leave. For Kabir the crowd became the enemy and once the battle lines were drawn, everything became easy for him. He drew himself straight, squared his shoulders, strode ahead, pulled the boy free and took out a handkerchief from his pocket to stem the flow of blood.

"Let him go," he said softly, though his voice was firm, as though he was a commander giving directions to his troops. "As he said, it was an accident. We all saw it; the bull charged at him and he fell down. The mutton flew from his hand."

But the crowd was not his set of troops who would disperse on receiving orders from him. This was a crowd that was getting restive and wanted to draw blood.

"*Abey tu kaun hai*?" asked someone belligerently. *Hey, who are you?*

Kabir turned to look at the questioner a trifle contemptuously. It was a puny little man whose head barely came up to Kabir's chest and who would have walked past him without angling for a fight, had they collided on a deserted street. But there was safety in numbers and the little man in a white striped shirt and dirty pyjamas knew it, too.

"*Yeh bhi Mussalman hai*," said someone, and a cry of agreement rose in the air. *He is also a Muslim*. The butcher's young boy was forgotten. All eyes were on the tall, fair-complexioned man with a stubble and close-cropped hair, wearing a blue and white pinstriped shirt and grey pants. He had become their target and he knew that it would take them only a few minutes to pelt him with stones and leave him half dead.

"*Mussalman*. How do you know?" asked another man.

"There is only one way to find out," sniggered someone in the crowd, and Kabir knew instantly what he meant. He too had watched the award-winning film *Mr and Mrs Iyer*. Someone tugged at his pants and he felt his stomach tighten into knots. Another man put an arm around his neck, perhaps looking for a *taweez* or lucky charm. Yet another person dipped a hand in his pant pocket, as if by siding with the poor butcher's boy Kabir had forfeited his right to privacy and dignity and had suddenly been transformed into public property. The man's probing fingers found a wallet, which had no driver's license or credit card. There were five crumpled 1,000-rupee notes in the wallet, which revealed nothing about his religion, but safeguarded his anonymity.

Someone pulled something off his neck, looked disappointed and exclaimed, *"Arre yeh to Christian hai." Oh, he is a Christian.*

Kabir looked with surprise at the gold chain around his neck, on which hung a cross with the name Terry engraved on it. For a moment he forgot how it had reached there. Another man pulled a handkerchief from his pocket and saw the word "Terry" embroidered on it. *"Haan, yeh Christian hai,"* he repeated, unable to hide his disappointment. *"Iska naam Terry hai." Yes, he is a Christian. His name is Terry.*

"Whoever he is, he is right," said a man in saffron robes. "Let him and the butcher's boy go. No religion preaches conflict or communal violence. No religion preaches hatred."

"But," argued the *halwai*, "the prasad has been defiled."

The saffron-clad swami smiled gently and said, "It is only five o'clock now. The *aarti* will take place only at eight o'clock. There is enough time to make the ladoos again."

Kabir began to breathe fully once the swami stopped speaking and the crowds began to disperse. So shaken was he that he breathed rapidly. He walked slowly, almost dragging his feet as he thought of the last meeting he had with Teresa—Terry for short.

It had been a painful encounter. Religion had come in the way of their feelings, an unexpected intruder, and an obstacle that he had not anticipated. She had raised her head, looked at him resolutely and said, "Kabir, I am sorry; we cannot get married."

"Why?" he had asked.

"Our religions are different."

Her reply had stunned him. Religion had never been an issue with them.

"Kabir," she had murmured, her voice low, "I am a Christian. I would like to baptise our children."

"It is understood that we will marry under the Special Marriages Act," interrupted Kabir.

"The Church will never accept our wedding until you convert," said Terry. "But you are an atheist. Our marriage will never work."

He had laughed upon hearing her. He was the child of a Hindu father and a Muslim mother. No wonder they had named him Kabir. He had grown up in a secular environment. Their policy had been "live and let live." His parents had celebrated Diwali and Eid with equal fervour. He empathised with everyone: Hindus, Muslims, Sikhs and Christians. His parents had left the choice of religion to him and he had preferred to embrace both. Just because he did not perform *namaaz* regularly or visit the temple every day did not mean he was atheist or agnostic. It was humanitarianism and not religion that had made him support the young butcher's boy.

Kabir had begun to protest that Terry was being difficult. During the five years he had known her, they had never seriously discussed religion. He had embraced Christianity as well and added Christmas to his list of celebrations. Then he saw the guilt in her eyes and guessed. He decided to call her bluff. He took her in his arms and muttered, "I love you so much, Terry; for your sake I am willing to convert."

"No," she said.

"Religion is just an excuse, isn't it, Terry? You have found someone else," he challenged.

"John," she admitted. "He is also a Christian. And he is an engineer who lives here. I met him when you were posted to Jodhpur. We love each other. I want to marry him."

"If only you had told me the truth," Kabir said, blinking back tears, "instead of trying to blame me for breaking up the relationship."

"I am sorry," she said. "I just didn't know how to." Then she removed the gold chain with the cross, which he had gifted to her on her birthday. It had her name engraved on it.

"Keep it, Terry," he said. "It's not an engagement ring."

"No, Kabir," she said resolutely. "It's over. Don't live on false hopes."

He had not been able to control himself. She had looked at him with horror. She had never seen him weep. She had no idea till then just how much he loved her. "Here, Kabir, don't cry," she had said, and shoving her handkerchief in his hand she had left hurriedly.

Since then he had been roaming aimlessly on the streets, trying to make his mind go blank to ease his pain. For hours he had been blaming her and trying to hate her. But her action, selfish as it was, had inadvertently saved his life. Major Kabir Khanna shrugged his shoulders. It was important to be alive. Love could come later.

# Cry, My Beloved Child

It's raining. I love rain. I love making paper boats and floating them on open drains. I love getting drenched and swinging my wet hair from side to side as the water dribbles down my back. I love the smell of mud, the richness and the fragrance of the rain-washed earth. I love the cry of the peacock as it breaks into a dance. It is so different from a baby's cry.

As if on cue, you start wailing. Your face puckers up. You lie on the cot, tiny and red-faced. Your hands are balled into little fists. Your eyes are charcoal black. They are not the colour of my eyes, hazel flecked with gold. Then whose? I do not know. I will never know.

But you are flesh of my flesh, blood of my blood. Your eyes screwed tight, as if shielding themselves from the harsh glare of the world. The nurse has come into the room. I know what she will tell me: "Lift up your blouse and feed the baby."

Feed you? Allow you to drain me completely? To sap my energy, and leave me exhausted, an empty shell of what I once was? For three days, I have withstood the pain of childbirth, the pain of the caesarian operation. I can't bear it any more.

"Sister, I can't feed him; take him away from me," I say. But no sound emanates from my mouth. Only I can hear my silent plea; no one else can. Am I dumb? Or is everyone here deaf?

Sister Nivedita enters the room. "Lift the child," she says persuasively, and my hands move to pick you up. "Feed it," she commands, and I obey instinctively. Nivedita. The name sounds familiar. Namita, Nivedita, Nivedita, Namita.

How do names matter, anyway? For me, everything is a blur, a haze. Sometimes I think I am losing my mind. My past is like a slate wiped clean. There is a medical name for my condition, but I forget what it is.

"It's trauma. It has resulted in loss of speech," the doctor had said. Perhaps she is right. Sister Nivedita stands beside me. She asks me eagerly, "Do you remember?"

"Remember me till I'm dead, dead, dead...oranges and lemons, sold for a penny," the ditty begins to resound in my brain. A picture swims in my mind of me wearing a blue pinafore and a white blouse, hair tied up in pigtails, jumping around the playground. Which school was it? The name eludes me. But I remember that it was just down the road, which was lined with *gulmohar* trees, whose crimson flowers in full bloom always reminded me of a forest fire.

My house, too, had a name. Yes, it is coming back to me. I too have a name. And a big white house with a courtyard, where Ma sliced up mangoes and put them out into the courtyard to dry, filling up the entire house with the aroma of the raw fruit. Large bottles of *aam ka achar* were then kept out in the sun till the green skin turned a deep yellow, and simply melted on one's tongue. I would steal the achar and eat dollops of it along with a crispy, six-layered paratha straight from the tawa.

Yes, the house exists. You, my dear child, will no longer be homeless. When I get out of this place, this sanatorium, or whatever they call it, you and I will go and look for our house.

We'll trudge along, with you nestling in the crook of my arms, and search for our house. Ma will be so happy when I get back. After Father died, she had no one but me for company.

You and I, my little one, share a similar destiny. I never saw my father. He died in an accident before I was born. And you will never know yours. But there is a difference between us. My father's photograph hangs in our drawing room wall. As Ma and I made garlands to wreathe his photograph, I could feel him smiling down benevolently at me. But you? What about you?

But wait; there is something wrong. I remember now that there will be no Ma at the gate. I last saw her covered in a white sheet, and I had heard the neighbours whisper, "What will happen to Namita?" Then Baba's relatives took charge of me. "Come to us," they wrote, "and make your home with us." So I left my home and went to them. "Will you be able to go to your uncle's home on your own?" Ravi Chacha, my neighbour, had asked me at the station. "Of course, Chacha," I had said, smiling through my tears, but feeling very lonely in the AC second-class train compartment.

The train was due to arrive in Kanpur at noon, but it had broken down en route. God knows when it would reach Kanpur.

"I hope you have someone to receive you at the station?" enquired a fellow passenger.

I hoped so, too, especially as the evening had melted into the night by the time the train arrived at the station. But there was no familiar face waiting for me in this unknown city, although I waited at the station for almost half an hour. Perhaps they had got tired of waiting and left. No scooter or taxi was willing to take me to my destination, as my uncle's house was very close to the station.

Dejectedly, I started walking out of the station with my small suitcase in my hand. I entered the alley which led to my uncle's house. I then saw them coming towards me. They appeared to be shadows that had suddenly detached themselves from the boundary wall outside the railway station and assumed demonic shapes.

They were four of them. They headed straight for me. Disoriented and fatigued by the long journey and sweltering heat, I wondered what they wanted from me. Then I saw them laugh and I knew. I prayed then that I should die. But I didn't. Not when they pulled me by my hand and dragged me, kicking and screaming. Not when they threw me on an old and sagging cot. Not when they put their smelly, sweaty hands on my mouth to smother my screams and to choke my cries. I struggled, I fought, I kicked, I bit, and cried some more. But there was no escape.

"After every night, however dark, there is a dawn," says Sister Nivedita. But she, in her white gown, dedicated to the love of God...what does she know of life, of its todays and tomorrows? What does she know of the pain, that tearing, searing pain, which is ripping me apart? What does she know of the humiliation and rage which is burning within me? There will be no escape and there will be no rescue, for there are no heroes in this world; there are only villains.

And I am left to die, day by day. No one understands my trauma. Not these white-gowned nuns who found me comatose and took me in. To nurse "the wonder that is growing within you" they had said. Did they not understand that all these months, while you were growing inside me, my son, I loathed you? I loathed the blood that mingled with mine to give you birth. But I could not tell them this. I had already drifted into a soundless world.

It was only when the police came for questioning me and asked me my name that I realised I had lost my voice as well as my memory. "Trauma," they said. I hated it, hearing but not being heard, screaming silent screams of anguish, not being able to remember my name.

But now, my child, I remember everything. I remember my childhood and my youth. I remember the dark alley into which the four men dragged me, the cot on which they threw me and the sweaty hands that clasped my mouth, almost smothering me, like this.

The vice-like grip on my throat, which bottled out my cries, like this.

My limp, silent form, like this.

"Sister, Nurse, Sister Nivedita, what's wrong? Why doesn't anyone come?" I shout.

Oh, Sister Nivedita is here. Why is she eyeing me so strangely? Why has she taken you from me? How did you get all those long, angry red weals on your throat? Why are your lips so waxen and pale? Why is your body so limp?

My son! You were crying so lustily just moments ago. Why have you stopped? Why are you silent now? Cry once, just once. Cry, my beloved child, cry.

# One Rotten Apple

The screeching of a van's brakes brought me to the window. I pulled the curtains apart and the burst of sunlight made me blink. A truck stood parked outside our apartment building. "We've got neighbours," I said, a note of enthusiasm creeping into my voice.

There was no reaction from Mum and Dad. Their heads bent, they were poring over the Scrabble board. "A seven-letter word, and that too on a triple-word score," said Mum, rubbing her hands in delight as she quickly made BISCUIT. Dad looked a little put off. She had won again. She usually did.

Ravish came into the drawing room at that time. "Mom, I want breakfast," he muttered. His voice sounded crabby. He had not slept the whole night. The law school entrance exams were around the corner.

"SYNTAX," Mum said, swooping upon the word TAX, which Dad had made. "SYNTAX on the triple-word score yet again." She let out a cry of delight.

"Mom," Ravish's voice was unnaturally loud, "I want breakfast."

"It's on the table," she said, her head still bent. "The cornflakes, apple, milk, sugar and orange juice."

"I want scrambled eggs," he insisted, his voice peevish.

I moved away from the window and walked into the kitchen. I put a frying pan on the stove top, broke two eggs into it, added milk, butter and salt, stirred it gently on a slow fire, and within minutes spooned it onto a plate along with two crisp toasts. Ravish wolfed it down appreciatively and said, "Thanks, *di*."

I shot a look of triumph at Ma. Successful career woman, successful wife, and lousy cook. At least this was one area where I was better than her.

"Stop crouching around the house like a panther in the wilds, Mita," ordered Ma, while putting another word on the board. Playing Scrabble was her way of relaxing and Dad, recently retired from the army, was pathetically grateful for her company during the weekends. I scowled and went back to the window.

The luggage was being unloaded outside our apartment building. A large fridge, probably GE, two LG air conditioners, double beds, a dressing table, a piano and kitchenware. I stood a little behind the curtain. I did not want to seem to be prying.

A Honda City stopped by the van. A man stepped out of the car. With dark glasses, he seemed to be of indeterminate age. An overgrown beard covered half his face. He was lithe, strong and muscular. I could imagine him jogging around Lodhi Gardens in shorts and a tee shirt, his muscles rippling. I wondered if his wife would step out after him. No one did.

"Bachelor." I did not realise I had said the word aloud.

"What?" asked Ma.

"Don't worry, Ma, it is not a seven-letter word," I muttered.

"Don't be silly." Ma shot me a stern look.

I thrust out my chin. Ma was warning me to keep away from the new neighbour. She had not forgotten Nishant; nor had she forgiven me. She still remembered the time when she walked into the house and found Nishant coming out of my bedroom. Out of a feeling of pique, I had not told her that I had called Nishant simply to change the bulb in my bedroom. I was happy to let her think the worst and simmer in anger.

"Don't worry, *di*," said Ravish, winking at me. "Our new neighbour will probably come to borrow a cup of sugar or milk, sooner or later."

Ravish was wrong; the neighbour did not come to see us under any pretext. I did meet him two days later when we were coming up the lift. He stood in the corner, his head down, as if he was warding us off. I looked at him, my eyes roaming across his face, or whatever little of it was visible.

Ma seemed annoyed at me for my open display of curiosity. But there was little she could do about it. Just as the door opened, he left without even a backward glance. His message to us was loud and clear: stay away.

"There is an air of mystery about him," I muttered, secretly wishing that we stayed on the eighth floor and not the third so that we could have been together in the lift for longer.

"Probably he is a small-time crook," Ma hazarded, making her dislike for him very evident.

"Small-time crooks do not live in our kinds of apartments," I argued. Dad had never stopped boasting that our four-bedroom luxury apartment had cost us one crore rupees.

For days I kept a watch on the neighbouring apartment. I had all the time in the world to do it. But I never saw any visitors coming to see him. He was clearly a recluse.

I was preparing for my CAT exam. Ma wanted me to do an MBA. "What else is there to do?" Ma's eyes spoke a lot.

"Not everyone is brilliant like you," I said, thrusting out my chin. "Some of us are average people like me."

But Ma, a senior vice president at a multinational company, would never be able to understand how a girl could be satisfied with being just a homemaker. Luckily, she was a realist and realised that the chances of my cracking the CAT were almost negligible. But it made a good conversational gambit. Ma's statement, "Mita is taking the CAT exam," explained to her friends why I was lounging around the house for months instead of doing something useful with myself.

Although I did not meet my mysterious neighbour for a while, I got regular updates on him from our bai. His bai and ours were friends, which was not surprising. All the bais who worked in the apartments were known to each other.

"All he does is drink," she disclosed, screwing up her nose in disgust, as though she could smell liquor around her. "He sits in the evening eating chicken tikka and drinking. He stares at the walls all the time. He does nothing. At times he sketches furiously, at other times he writes furiously. He does not leave the house. He is like a prisoner."

"A graphic designer or an architect," I surmised. "That would explain the sketching and the writing. Or a writer-cum-illustrator," I added as an afterthought.

"Perhaps he has been a prisoner, or perhaps he is not used to freedom," Ma murmured.

"True." Dad's voice was mild; he seldom disagreed with Ma. "What do you think he is?"

"A small-time crook?" Ma could not hide the contempt from her voice.

"Perhaps he has a disease, or perhaps he is dying of cancer." Ravish's interruption surprised me. He took an apple, polished it with the edge of his tee shirt and crunched it loudly between his teeth.

"Can't be true," interjected Ma. "He looks healthy—disgustingly so."

Ravish gave Ma a telling look. He hadn't finished as yet. "Or AIDS," he concluded.

Ma's eyes began to glint. "That is a distinct possibility," she said with relish.

Perhaps it was this conversation that stoked my curiosity further. So when I found the neighbour's door ajar, I gave it a knock and walked in. He was sitting on a rocking chair, rocking himself slowly like an old man, with his back towards the wall. He was oblivious to my presence. I walked in and stood before him till he was forced to look at me. "I wanted to borrow…some sugar," I almost said, but stopped myself at the right time. I was carrying no sugar bowl. "The newspaper," I substituted. "We get *The Indian Express* at home." I had already espied *The Times of India* lying on the sofa. He handed me the newspaper; the gesture signified dismissal. It robbed me of an excuse to stay on in his house.

I went out and stared at him. I realised that I would need to borrow the newspaper every day. It seemed a good excuse for seeing him. The next day I knocked at his door boldly after I saw the bai leave. "I wanted to borrow the newspaper," I requested. "I am preparing for the CAT exams."

He continued to stare at the wall, as if he could see a unique mosaic on it, invisible to others' eyes. He did not even turn when I said, "Thank you," and closed the door behind me.

The third day there was a knock on our door around 11 am, and I saw with dismay his bai standing with a copy of *The Times of India*. His message was plain: do not intrude. But I chose to be obtuse. After going through *The Delhi Times* quite avidly I trotted off to his apartment. I found the door ajar once again. I was sure he had not heard his bai leave. I knocked perfunctorily and then walked in. He seemed surprised to see me.

"I had sent you the newspaper," he said.

"I came to return it," I retorted.

"If it is not too much of a bother, just push it under the door, will you?" he asked sarcastically. This was the longest sentence he had spoken to me. I would have called it progress, but for the fact that I now had no reason to see him.

For the next week or so I had no news of him. Then his bai, Mamta, took a week's leave to go to her village. "How would he cope?" I wondered, although I did not have the courage to barge into his house again. I knew the answer to it soon enough. Delivery boys from Domino's Pizza, Subway and McDonald's began frequenting our apartment block regularly. I had no doubt as to where all the food was going.

A fortnight later as I was passing by his apartment, I found him rasping loudly. The door was ajar. The pizza delivery boy had just left and I was sure that our neighbour had no time to close the door. I stopped outside and listened. When he coughed once again I barged in. His face was completely flushed. I put my hand on his forehead. It was burning with fever. "Where do you keep the thermometer?" I asked briskly.

This time he did not argue. "In the bathroom," he said a bit weakly.

"And paracetamol?" I asked.

He gestured towards the dining table. I took his temperature and was shocked to see that it was 103 degrees Fahrenheit. I made him swallow two paracetamols and then asked him if I could ring up his doctor.

"Will you?" he asked humbly. "Dr Shroff's number is in my diary." He propped himself on his elbow and took out his diary from his pocket.

There was no telephone anywhere, but I saw his cell phone on the table. I picked it up and dialled the doctor's number. The phone kept ringing, but no one answered. "Probably a wrong number," I surmised, and dialled again. This time I got the doctor's clinic. I handed over the phone to the neighbour, and the doctor, obviously a friend of his, decided to drop by.

I was with my neighbour when Dr Shroff appeared, and if he was surprised to see me he did not show it.

"Chest infection," he diagnosed, "Aloo, I am leaving you some antibiotics."

"Aloo?" I giggled to myself.

The neighbour glared at me. Dr Shroff chuckled and said sorry, although he displayed no sorrow whatsoever.

"Aloo," I thought exultantly. I now knew his nickname. I had still to learn his name and surname. His house had no name plate on it. He seemed almost paranoid about keeping his identity a secret. I realised I would not be able to learn my neighbour's identity from Dr Shroff. "If he can get some good home-cooked food and medicines, he shall be fine," the doctor told me, possibly misreading our relationship.

I nodded. That evening I returned to the neighbour's apartment with a bowl of home-made soup and some khichri and left it on his table. I would have loved to spoon-feed him, but I was a realist and did not push my luck. His illness gave me the opportunity to show off my culinary skills.

The next day he opened the door and asked, "What have you brought for me?"

"*Sabudana* khichri," I said, entering his house.

"*Sabudana*," he blew up. "I hate it."

Tears sprang up in my eyes. I began to rush out of the door.

"Wait," he said, getting hold of my hand and pulling me inside. "Serve me the khichri," he ordered.

"Eat it yourself." The words were on my lips; thankfully, I did not utter them. I spooned the khichri onto a plate and soon found him eating it with his fingers.

"Delicious," he murmured. "You are a whiz cook, kid."

Kid! Just how old was he? 30, 35 or 40? I had no clue. But his words filled me with pride.

"Since you are bent upon playing nursemaid," he said, his smile taking the sting out of his words, "let me confess that I hate brinjal, pumpkin and bitter gourd."

I smiled. Those were my least favourite vegetables as well. We had something in common, after all. "Tell me what you want to eat tomorrow," I asked.

"Can you make aloo parathas?" he said.

"No," I vetoed, "you are ill. Aloo *ka* parathas are out."

He made a face at me. The next day when I came I said conspiratorially, "I have got you aloo *ka* parathas without oil."

He grabbed the plate from my hand, tore a large piece of the paratha and stuffed it into his mouth. He munched it happily and after polishing it off said, "You have magic in your fingers."

The next afternoon, when I arrived at his house carrying pasta in tomato sauce, Dr Shroff was already present. "Mita, you are a miracle worker," he said appreciatively. "Your patient's fever is down and he is much better."

My heart sank at the thought that my neighbour would not need me any more. I had come to look forward to his dependence on me.

He surprised me by saying, "I still need home-cooked food for some more days, at least till my bai returns."

"You must be an excellent cook, if he relishes your cooking," grinned the doctor. "Your patient is a gourmand."

This revelation gave me the incentive to experiment with the meals I planned to bring him. For once I was glad Mom was the vice president of an MNC and returned late from work. I had all the time to myself and no one questioned me about what I was cooking. On the fifth day I made him some Thai chicken curry and jasmine rice.

"Are you a mind reader?" he asked wonderingly. "I love Thai food. It's my favourite."

"It's my favourite, too," I confessed.

On the sixth day his bai returned and I realised that I no longer had any reason for seeing him.

A few days later, when I was unable to restrain myself any longer, I dropped in to see him. He was sitting on the rocking chair and rocking himself slowly. He looked at me without recognition. He seemed to have forgotten about the past week.

"How are you today?" I asked him, but he looked at me as if he was seeing me for the first time. I felt a pang of disappointment. We were back to where we had started. He had become a stranger once again.

"What do you want?" he asked, his voice brusque.

"You know I am taking the CAT exams," I said. "I was hoping that you could teach me." It sounded like a pretty weak excuse, even to my own ears.

"The only thing I can teach you is about death; I can teach you nothing else," he said abruptly. There was no point in carrying on a conversation with him, I realised, and left.

A week later I heard his rasping cough and, finding his apartment door open, I walked in without knocking. He frowned when he saw me. "Why do you keep coming here, Mita?" he asked.

"I don't know," I admitted. I did not know myself what drew me to him repeatedly. Was it sheer curiosity? Was it an unknown attraction? Was I falling in love with him?

"I do," he challenged. "I know why you come."

"Why?" My eyes widened.

"Because..." he said.

A minute later, I left his room crying. It was unfortunate that Ma came out of the lift just then and saw me rushing into our house.

"Where are you coming from, as though the devil himself was at your heels," Ma asked me sharply.

"Nowhere," I muttered.

But Ma had seen that our neighbour's door was ajar. She figured that I had returned from there. She barged into his house without even a perfunctory knock at the door and said in a loud voice, "Let me warn you once and for all, just keep away from my daughter."

My face burnt with humiliation as I imagined him retorting, "It is your daughter who cannot keep away from me." But he said nothing. He continued to look through her, as though she didn't exist, and Ma confessed that even she was intimidated by his cold stare.

Three days later he left his apartment. I did not know when he had left but I saw a van taking away his furniture. No one knew where he had disappeared. The next day the maid came with a sheaf of newspapers. "Sahib said you may find them useful," she murmured.

Ma looked at me meaningfully while I muttered something about needing TOI for my CAT exams. "You could have subscribed to the newspaper yourself," she admonished as she picked up the newspaper on the top of the pile and began reading it.

The newspaper was opened onto a page where our neighbour had doodled a lot. He had drawn a long line against the margin of the story. Ma gave but a cursory glance to the main story of a woman who had drowned her two children in the bathtub; the woman had been considered mentally unstable and committed to an institution for life. After all, who was interested in a woman?

Ma's eyes were focused on the next item, the story of a man who was suspected of murdering his wife, whom he had suspected of infidelity. He was given the benefit of the doubt as there were no eyewitnesses and the evidence against him was circumstantial. The man had left Kolkata, unable to withstand the hostility of his neighbours and acquaintances, and moved to Delhi. Ma was convinced that the man was our mysterious neighbour. "Alok Virmani," she said ruminatively. "That is his name. Now you know who he is," she continued. "He must be this man. He must have left the city once again. I had warned you not to go to his apartment."

I did not pay any attention to what she was saying. I remembered him muttering, "I know what you want," and pinning me against the wall, looking at me with tortured eyes. "You don't know anything about me, Mita; you do not know you are playing with fire."

I had closed my eyes and felt his lips cracked and salty on mine, felt his beard graze my face, the bristles hurting me. He raised his head suddenly, as if to clear it, and his whispered, "Get out, get out of here, will you?"

I had stroked my bruised lips with my fingers and was shaken, both by his touch and the emotions he invoked within me. I rushed from his house, as though the devil himself was at my heels. Now I realised what he meant when he had said, "You do not know anything about me."

Alok...Aloo...It all fitted in. We had not heard of the case because we had been away for a family holiday to Singapore and had missed the TV news and the newspaper reports. All I felt now was loathing for him, for what he had done, and contempt for myself, for falling for a criminal like him.

I would never have known the truth about him but for a sheer chance. One Sunday, Ma was channel surfing during a two-minute break while watching a serial, when she switched to a show where they showed the woman I had read about in *The Times of India*—the Mumbai resident who had drowned her two children in the bathtub. On the screen she sat on a hospital bed, her eyes unseeing, fixed on a large family photograph on the wall. The cameras zoomed on the photograph and there was no mistaking it: sitting with her and her two sons was her husband. It was our mystery neighbour. "Mannan Aluwalia," the announcer disclosed.

Aloo! Aluwalia! Once again everything fell into place. His inability to live in his old house, his need to escape from old friends and acquaintances and old memories, his coming to Delhi from Mumbai and shifting to our apartment building almost incognito, his staring into space for long intervals, his abrupt sentences, his long silences, his glazed eyes, the bottles of whisky and his need to be loved.

For days afterwards I sat in the Delhi Public Library and read about the murder in the old newspapers. I read about his wife, a schizophrenic who took her two boys for a bath and then drowned them in the tub. Mannan had returned from work to find his wife sitting beside her two dead children and asking him, "Why don't they laugh any more, Mannan, and why don't they cry?" Suddenly he had lost everything he had held dear, his wife and his two sons. I recalled that there was so much sadness in his eyes and raw passion in his voice when he had said, "Mita, you are playing with fire."

"You did the young man a grave injustice," Dad told Ma, a mild reprimand in his voice. Ma bristled with anger initially and then admitted, "I was wrong about him and I would like to say sorry to him, but no one knows how to contact him, no one knows where he's gone."

I did not admit in front of Ma that I knew how to contact him. That day when he had been down with raging fever, on the pretext of ringing up the doctor, I had first given a blank call to my own cell phone and then claimed that I had connected with a wrong number. I had got the doctor on the second ring.

I closed my eyes and thought about him. I still knew very little about him. He was years older than me. He had been the victim of a grave tragedy. He had built a wall around him, which no one had been able to penetrate. I had tried my best to do it, but had failed. He was possibly attracted to me. Or maybe he was just lonely. He did not even like me very much and he had made that abundantly clear. But he needed someone in his life who could help him start all over again. He would no doubt rebuff me, but I was willing to risk it. He had warned me that I was playing with fire, but I was prepared to have my fingers burnt. I went to my room, picked up my mobile and dialled.

# Death Wish

The day Rishi was born was the day I died. Only I did not know it then. I exulted in the news of his birth. I beamed with happiness. I let each aching muscle of mine do a little jig. I pirouetted with glee. It was better than having won the lottery. I had given birth to a son. It was the equivalent of having reached heaven, or nirvana—salvation. I mentally somersaulted. I waltzed in my dreams. I kick-boxed. I did complex mathematical calculations in my head. I smirked. The birth of a male child had catapulted me into an exclusive club.

With her smouldering eyes and sharp tongue, my mother-in-law now seemed like a fire prematurely extinguished. The joy of having a grandchild and that too a grandson, after seven years of waiting, outweighed my being swept into prominence.

Sandeep smiled. Suddenly he loved me, even with rolls of flesh around my waist. He had never shown such tenderness to me, even when we had just got married. I rolled on the bed, trying to catch up on sleep. My mother, wearing a white sanitised saree, stretched out her legs in the bathroom, put Rishi astride them, gently poured soapy water on him, washed him, and then, enveloping him in a large towel, scrubbed him dry. I saw her slip him into an old frock, which had belonged to my cousin's child, in keeping with tradition, and watched her with fascination. Would I ever master the art of holding his slippery flesh and giving him a bath?

"You will learn," said Mother indulgently. "It comes naturally to women." Perhaps she was right. But to most women motherhood too comes easily. It had not come easily to me.

It had taken me seven years. Seven years of people watching my flat abdomen, my mother-in-law with accusation, Sandeep with scepticism and the neighbours with interest. An abdomen that refused to balloon. A womb that remained empty.

I spent seven years loving others' kids...and hating them. Envying women with pink doll daughters with sticky fingers and candy-flossed lips, women with boys who had marbles in their hands and frogs in their pockets, women who had infants stuck to their breasts like overfed leeches, and men who pushed prams with gurgling babies inside. Seven years of oscillation between hope and despair, crossing dates on calendars, taking my basal body temperature, finding the right date and realising that fertility was not a word one associated with land, crops and harvest alone, but a woman's body, too. I spent years taking fertility drugs and steroids for my fibroids, and found myself beginning to balloon. I spent years living with my bouts of depression and surges of confidence, finding no one to share my thoughts with, and seeing myself as a huge failure. I saw the word 'failure' writ large on imaginary neon signs and billboards, because I had failed Sandeep, because I had been something less than a woman.

I spent seven years dusting crystal figurines, polishing Belgian glass, cleaning tarnished silverware, placing rich brocade saris woven with threads of real gold between sheets of muslin cloth and storing them in the almirah. I spent seven years making potpourri of dried twigs, crushed flowers and aromatic leaves, keeping out woollen clothes in the sun, storing them in big black trunks with mothballs, slicing mangoes to make pickles, grinding pulses to make *baris* and papaddams, drying green chillies soaked with yogurt out in the sun. Anything to take my mind away from my washboard stomach and barren insides. But the seven years' drought had ended at last.

A month after Rishi's birth, we held a puja for him in our house, which reeked of incense sticks, sandalwood, jasmine and musk, camphor, crushed roses and lemon leaves. I sat cross-legged on a silken coverlet with Rishi on my lap, his soft black hair covering his head, his eyes shut tight, and his tiny hands clenched into fists. I felt a stirring in my engorged breasts and smiled at the sight of a telltale leak on my blouse that glorified my motherhood.

The priest, clad in white, began his complex mathematical calculations that would foretell Rishi's future, and as he mumbled, I became a little imp who jumped across the room into the minds of men and women, ferreting out their innermost thoughts. "She has done it. The barren woman has given birth to a son, someone to take the family line forward." "Who would have thought it to be possible, that too after seven years?"

"It is her own child, no suspicious business here; I know the midwife." The imp continued to dance on the heads of people. I had no inkling then that something was wrong. There was no checklist against which I could check Rishi.

"He doesn't turn," my mother-in-law with her smouldering eyes said one day. I should have heard warning bells then, but I didn't. Later when I went to the district hospital, my hand protectively holding Rishi's neck, the doctor asked me, "Doesn't he hold up his neck? How old is he?"

"Four months," I said, not noticing his pursed lips and deepening frown.

He handed me a list of milestones. "Keep track of the time when he achieves these," he ordered.

It took me six months to confirm that something was indeed wrong. He could not hold up his neck. He could not turn. He could not sit up. He could not crawl. The list was growing.

All he did was stare at the ceiling, saliva dribbling down his mouth, or wet the sheets. I should have guessed when he nibbled at my breasts listlessly. I should have guessed when he did not recognise me.

The diagnosis should not have come as a shock to me. I do not know the medical name for it, but the truth was that he suffered from severe physical and mental retardation. A vegetable. That is what he was and that is what he would remain. He would never play football with Sandeep. He would never go fishing with him. He would never graduate from college, never hold a job—any job. He would remain bed ridden and shackle me to his cot for the rest of my life. Sandeep gaped, his eyes widening, as the horror of the diagnosis registered. My mother-in-law's eyes smouldered some more.

"There must be some treatment," I babbled incoherently, spittle flying from my mouth and landing on Sandeep's shirt, "if not here, then in the USA, or Europe. Everything has a cure these days, just about everything. We live in the age of miracles. You must ask for leave. We can go abroad for his treatment."

Sandeep recoiled in horror. Rishi was an insult to his manhood. He was the result of a defective chromosome or gene. The scientist in Sandeep quailed at the thought.

"Among the ancient Greeks," said Sandeep's crusty, aged, shrivelled-up boss, masticating on a pencil end, "when a disabled child was born, he was left in the forest by the father."

Sandeep shivered, his eyes widening at the thought of wolves and foxes, tigers and lions, tearing the infant limb from limb, chewing on infant bones, leaving behind blood and gore. Sandeep did not say anything to his boss, but hung his head in shame. I had failed him.

I did it all. Fasted on Tuesdays and Thursdays. Stopped eating fish and meat on Mondays and Saturdays. Gave up sour foods on Fridays. I did anything and everything I could, just so that a miracle could happen. I walked barefoot to the temples that dotted the town, prostrated myself before a pantheon of gods, did penance for past sins, fed priests, orphans and street urchins, hoping for the miracle of Rishi raising his head and walking one day.

But the gods remained deaf to my pleas. As did Sandeep. Rishi had become a chasm that divided us. From being his beloved wife, I had become an untouchable. Every night, I put a tentative hand across the bed towards Sandeep. But he remained implacable. However, the night before he had to go to London he turned towards me and took me with a fervour that surprised me. I reeled under his passion and craved his touch, his body on mine, crushing me under his weight, his lips bruising mine, his hands boldly claiming possession over me. I forgot everything, Rishi, his mental state, and our own future. I only lived that moment. At last I drifted off to sleep, waking up when it was time for Sandeep to leave.

After the car had left for the airport, I drifted off to sleep once again, waking up only when the sunlight had flooded the room. It was then that I noticed Rishi lying soundlessly, his body still, his lips blue.

"Crib death," I said to the doctor on his arrival, "he died while he was asleep on his cot." I remember I had read about it in Dr Spock's book.

The doctor looked at me strangely. "In India we do not have crib deaths," he countered as he examined Rishi's body.

"Babies sleep on the bed with their parents. Someone pressed the pillow and smothered him until he died." Someone did it. He never named the "someone".

"It could have been anyone. Just anyone," I blabbered. But Sandeep had left before dawn and my mother-in-law had left for the temple in the morning. It could only have been me.

Still, the doctor did not say anything. He sat primly with his hands on his lap, his lips drawn in a straight line and his eyebrows beetled into a frown.

"No," I wanted to shout, "It was not me." But I was afraid that, like Pinocchio, my nose would grow longer with every lie I uttered. "He was my son," I murmured, but my voice faltered and my eyes said that I was glad he was dead. The doctor should have been glad too. It had all been for the best. Now Sandeep and I could start all over again.

But the doctor thought otherwise. "It is a murder," muttered the doctor, who thought it his duty to inform the police that someone had smothered the baby. Before I knew it, I was put into a police jeep and sent to the police lockup.

"What happened?" asked the lawyer, whom Sandeep had engaged out of a sense of duty. "Did you...?"

"Did I what?" Did I pick up a pillow and hold it to his face till he stopped breathing? Did I hold him tight in my dreamless sleep and snuff out his life? Did I roll over him by mistake and crush him beneath my weight? Or did Sandeep do it when he was groaning in passion? Had he crushed poor Rishi that night? Or had his passion been a part of an elaborate plan to smother Rishi to death? Was he smothering Rishi while I was drowning in his passionate lovemaking?

My mother-in-law, with her smouldering eyes, watched me being bundled into the police jeep and smiled. She knew she would find someone else for Sandeep, someone buxom, with fleshy thighs and heavy child-bearing hips, who would bear not one, not two, but many fine sons, tall and sturdy, who would hold up their necks at two months, sit up in five months, turn completely at six months, crawl at seven months, walk at twelve months, talk at one-and-a-half years and graduate from Harvard Business School at twenty-five years. Sons who would not lie salivating on the bed, amidst soiled and wet sheets.

"You will learn in time," Ma had said, laying to rest my doubts about raising Rishi. Had I learnt about his condition in time, I could have done something. Eaten raw papaya or sesame seed sweetmeats, foods that cause miscarriage; driven at breakneck speed on potholed, un-tarred, abortion roads; rolled down the staircase. But I had not known.

Now I lie in the cell, staring at the ceiling, wondering about the trial. I feel abandoned. Sandeep has not come to see me after returning to India. Nor has my mother-in-law. They have not arranged bail for me. They must be relieved. They are self-righteous and sanctimonious or they pretend to be. Murder is a non-bailable offence. They wish to have nothing to do with a murderer. But I know they must be relieved. I continue to stare at the ceiling and the walls. I can see slight cracks on the wall, or maybe they are the cobwebs. Rishi is dead, and very soon I may die. Or maybe I will continue to live in this cell until I do. But I know it was all over for me months ago.

The day Rishi was born was the day I died.

# The Greedy Girl

"Nothing good ever comes out of being greedy." I remember my *dadi* repeating it again and again while admonishing me as a child. "Learn self-restraint," she would mutter. "After all, you are a girl."

But all her lectures made no difference to me. Neither her admonitions nor my mother's rebukes ever registered in my brain. I was greedy, and unabashedly so. However, at least my *chachi* felt that something good came out of it.

Chachi was my father's younger brother's wife. She was universally disliked because she had done the unthinkable: walked out of our ancestral home and broken up our joint family. Surprisingly, Chacha, six feet tall and well built, had followed her meekly like a little lamb.

"She must be a sorceress," Dadi had lamented when Chachi left home. "She has done *jadu tona* on my son."

No one ever knew how the always-volatile, self-willed and headstrong Chacha had turned so docile. It wasn't as if Chachi was a beauty, or an heiress, or even moderately rich. She was five feet and six inches tall.

"Too tall," Ma had observed, critically, on seeing the photograph accompanying the marriage proposal. She had a dusky complexion with high cheekbones and a sharp aquiline nose. "Like a hawk," Ma had sniggered once again. Chachi had big eyes, but even here, Dadi found fault with her. "They are too huge for her face," she used to say.

I always wondered why they had even entertained her marriage proposal for Chacha if she had been so unsuitable. As for me, it was Chachi's hair that fell like a black curtain over her back that really captivated me. When she oiled it and tied it into plaits she reminded me of Rapunzel. But whenever she left it loose, it reminded me of black clouds before a storm.

But one day, soon after their marriage, I learnt that things between her and Chacha had changed. Chacha had been selected for the Indian Police Service.

"It's a powerful job," boasted Dadaji with a great deal of pride. Chacha would virtually be the king of the district, claimed Raghu Mama, a family friend. Everyone in the family was happy for Chacha and Chachi.

But it was too good to last. Soon Dadi began complaining that Choti Bahu had brought no dowry. After some time, even Dadaji began grumbling. "It was agreed," I heard him muttering, "that if he qualified in the civil service examinations, his in-laws would give us a car."

Chachi merely tossed her head and walked away every time she heard my grandparents begin their litany of complaints. They had been married for six months, she countered, and therefore, if Chacha had got a better job after marriage, well, it was because she'd brought him luck. I could never understand all this grown-up talk, although I heard it repeatedly.

As a nine-year-old, I always admired the sarees Chachi wore. I knew that her almirah was full of them. I also loved the diamond-studded *mangalsutra* she wore. I loved to jump on her double bed, which had such soft feather-weight mattresses that I could fall asleep the moment my head touched the fluffy pillow. When Chachi was not in her room, I loved to sit on the stool and try out the perfumes that adorned her dressing table.

But it was the goodies in Chachi's cupboard that I found irresistible. She kept jars full of roasted peanuts, cashew nuts and chocolate cookies in her cupboard, but I liked the *aam papad*, which her parents sent especially for her, the best. After I had indulged in much coaxing and pleading she would cut out a small piece, the size of a postage stamp, and give it to me, and she would explain that since the *aam papad* came from Kolkata, she did not want to exhaust her supplies until replenishments came.

Relations between Ma and Chachi deteriorated quickly when Ma once openly criticised Chachi for not helping in the housework and for spending hours dressing up or sleeping. Chachi was not one to take insults quietly. She retaliated quickly and said that at least she remained in the house when her husband was away on training in the police academy. She was not like Ma, who took advantage of her husband's posting outside Delhi to frequent Raghu Mama's house alone, on the pretext that it was en route to the mandir that she visited daily. And what, insinuated Chachi, was Raghu Mama's exact relationship with Ma? He was only a family friend, after all! Ma seethed with rage at her accusation but could not come up with a suitable rejoinder.

Meanwhile, Dadi had a big showdown with Chachi when she virtually accused Chachi of stealing the diamond ring that she had left in the bathroom while taking her bath.

Now it was Chachi's turn to get infuriated. "Me? Are you accusing me, the great-granddaughter of a Rai Bahadur, of stealing a ring?" she snarled, reminding me of a Royal Bengal tigress. Chachi alleged that this was Dadi's plan to get rid of her, so that she could get Chacha married once again. She claimed that this was nothing but blackmail. It was a disguised attempt of Dadi to seek dowry. The ring was never found and although Dadi wanted to notify the police, Dadaji and Ma intervened, and for the sake of family honour, the matter was dropped.

Chachi began to be treated like a pariah in her own house. Everyone ignored her. Ma told us not to speak to Chachi or go to her room. But one Sunday, when Chachi had gone for her bath, I could not resist the temptation of entering it. I opened Chachi's cupboard, and stood admiring all the goodies in it. Just when I had taken out a slab of *aam papad* I heard footsteps. There was no place to hide except under the bed. In a trice I slid under it only to discover that Chachi had filled the place with big suitcases. Although the space between the suitcases was horribly cramped, I managed to squeeze myself in. Chachi entered the room, singing to herself. Her hair, covered with a white towel, was tied into a big turban to soak the water.

She removed the towel and began to brush her hair vigorously. As usual I was fascinated as I watched her undertake this ritual. After drying her hair, she lay down on her bed. I hoped that she would sleep soon, for only then could I escape. I knew that it would be difficult to crawl out without making a noise.

I waited for about 10 minutes and then began edging out from beneath her bed like a soldier escaping from an enemy camp. Suddenly I heard footsteps. They paused at the door and then seemed to wait there interminably. By this time Chachi had begun to snore gently. God, I thought angrily, now I will have to wait much longer.

Then the feet, accompanied by the gentle ringing of *ghungroos*, walked around the bed. There was a sound of something being sprayed, followed by a familiar click, and then the footsteps were gone.

I lay terror-stricken beneath the bed, wondering what was happening, when I saw big orange flames lick the bed. "Chachi!" I called out, but by then Chachi was fast asleep. "Chachi," I shouted once again, my voice shrill.

Then I tried to crawl out but found myself stuck between the suitcases. "Chachi!" I bellowed. Chachi got up in a rush but, still disoriented, could not make out where the screams were coming from. She pulled me out when I thought I was about to collapse but the burning leg of the bed scorched a portion of my face.

"It doesn't matter, Simi," said Chachi later on. "Don't you know even the beautiful moon is scarred? Don't worry, you can always hide the scar by keeping your hair open, and letting it fall on your face. When you grow up, you can undergo plastic surgery."

Chachi didn't know who caused the fire but she created a huge fuss about it. Her shouts brought the entire family to her door.

"It must have been an accident," muttered Dadaji.

"You must have left incense sticks burning inside your room," murmured Dadi.

When Chachi insisted that the kerosene could not have come onto the bed on its own, they dismissed her story as a mere fabrication. No one paid any heed to me and my story, as I was just a child.

That evening Chachi coaxed the entire story out of me. I told her the sequence of events as faithfully as I could.

"Are you sure you didn't recognise the person who sprayed the kerosene onto the bed?" she urged.

"Chachi, I had almost dozed off," I told her, "since you were taking so long to sleep. All I heard was footsteps. I didn't see the person who did it. I only saw the feet."

"It must have been your Dadi," said Chachi with certainty. "She hates my guts. But there is no way I can prove it."

The same evening Chachi phoned Chacha and the very next morning he came home. Chacha, who after joining the police force had begun eyeing everyone with suspicion, did not want to take sides.

"I don't want to make a police case out of it," said Chachi. "After all, your folks are involved. But I won't stay here for even one more day. Who knows, the next time there may be no Simi to save me."

"I'm sorry, Chachi, for being greedy, and for stealing your *aam papad*," I said.

"I'm glad you were greedy," she said simply. "But for you I may well have been dead."

That evening Chachi and Chacha left our ancestral home for good.

In this hullabaloo everyone had forgotten about me, except Ma. "Who will marry you?" she kept repeating. "With that scar on your face? God has punished you for being greedy. Without plastic surgery on your face, no one will even look at you!"

I quailed at her outburst, but did not have the courage to ask her if this was God's way of punishing her as well.

For I may have omitted to tell Chachi about the anklets, but I had recognised the feet. I had heard the sound of the anklets for years when Ma woke me up every morning.

# Judge Not

The result of the DNA test is out. I stand vindicated. Relief seeps into my body slowly. I feel exultant, but my face remains impassive. I can see the shamefaced look on Shyamlee's face, which droops like a wilted rose. I cannot help feeling triumphant.

The head of SATYA, the NGO that spearheaded the smear campaign against me, has already tendered a written apology to me. Media persons surround me right now. They want a "byte" from me. I have only one thing to say to them. "Justice delayed is justice denied," I lament, referring obliquely to my reputation which, once pristine, has now become sullied, thanks to the mud which has stuck to me like an adhesive. More eyes are lowered hastily, more faces look guilty, and more shoulders become hunched. I walk away, my shoulders erect, and my head held high.

Back in the house I go into my study and put down my head on the study table. I hadn't admitted to myself or anyone else how tense I had been all this time. For me this past one month had been a veritable nightmare. Thankfully, it is finally over. I am a free man. I can breathe once again.

I shut my eyes tightly. I do not open my eyes even when I hear the jingle of bangles and the rattling of a tray. Shyamlee stands before me, the tea tray in hand. "I am glad it is over, Vivek; I always knew in my heart that this was not true," she says.

Bringing the tea tray is her peace offering. She could have asked anyone to bring me my tea. This is her unspoken way of saying, "I am sorry." Words, these are merely words. I can see the guilt in her eyes, but no remorse. If anything, I see the regret that her suspicions about me did not come true. Sometimes I wonder if the reason she had brought Nandita into our house was to pose a temptation before me and to see me succumb to it, just as she had.

Five years ago, I had caught Shyamlee in an embrace with my cousin Satish.

"Satish took me by surprise," she stuttered, while Satish hung his head and said nothing in his defence. I did not say anything. My silence was her punishment—a punishment that began that day and continues till today. Abstinence I could practice, if Gandhiji could.

Shyamlee could not understand my behaviour. "You treat me like a fallen woman," she stammered. "It was only an embrace."

She was right. I had witnessed only an embrace. But it had happened on the terrace, at 11.30 at night. And I saw it only by accident, because I came out to have a breath of fresh air, a gesture totally uncharacteristic of me.

Shyamlee knew that once I entered the study and began working on my judgements, I never came back to my room before 1.30 am. What had made me feel uneasy that day? Was it the rich meal she had served that night, the mutton pasanda, the *rajma*, and the biryani cooked in honour of Satish's arrival? Or was it a premonition of disaster? I do not know. All I saw on the terrace was a couple in a tight embrace, as though moulded into one. I thought it was my college-going daughter Vidya, as I entered the terrace. The figures sprang apart and I saw

Shyamlee and Satish. I had no idea for how long they had been on the terrace. I did not know what had preceded it. And I had no idea what would have followed if I had not intruded.

"It was only an embrace," muttered Shyamlee later.

"I have asked for no explanation," I said.

"You know what I mean. You have not touched me for three months," she quivered.

The three months turned to six months, to a year, to three years and then to five years. If the incident had taken place at a party, I may have understood. But not forgiven. I am conservative and I am not ashamed of the fact.

"I do not know what preceded the embrace," I said at last.

She blanched on hearing my words. "Satish took me by surprise and kissed me. It does not mean anything," she murmured softly.

But when I closed my eyes I could only see two figures, glued together, their arms entwined, their bodies touching, and one of them happened to be my wife. I wondered if, half an hour before, they had been lying on the terrace, Satish and Shyamlee, secure in the knowledge that I was locked up in my study. Had I been too late and was the embrace the final goodbye? Or was it the prelude? I did not know and I no longer wanted to know. Shyamlee was 10 years younger than me. And as the wife of a supreme court judge she enjoyed a great deal of liberty. But surely she understood the difference between liberty and license. I simply adopted abstinence as a way of life. Soon it became a habit that was not difficult to adhere to.

I think that when Shyamlee was asked by the short-stay home, a home for homeless women, to provide a home to Nandita, who was mute and mentally challenged, she agreed to the suggestion immediately with the idea of providing temptation. When Nandita first entered our home, I was taken aback. She was a beauty. Shyamlee had gone the whole hog to get a Menaka to tempt Vishwamitra.

"I will not allow her inside my house," I insisted.

"Our house," Shyamlee began and then, seeing the implacable expression on my face, decided to keep quiet. "Fine," she retorted, "she will stay not inside, but in our outhouse."

She got the outhouse of our spacious bungalow cleaned up for Nandita. I laughed as I thought of the Aishwarya Rai lookalike staying in our ramshackle outhouse. Nandita helped in maintaining the garden, which was Shyamlee's pride. She cooked her own food. Twice a week she went off to the home for homeless women. I did not have to see her at all.

Vidya laughed when she saw me shun Nandita. "Our Father who art in Heaven…lead us not into temptation," she chanted naughtily.

Kartik, our 17-year-old son, who was studying in Mayo College, Ajmer, came home for the holidays and seemed equally amused by my aversion to her.

Three months later while returning from the supreme court, I saw Nandita vomiting outside our house. It upset me to find the entrance to my house reeking of vomit. When winter was over and Nandita removed the shawls she had draped herself with, I said dispassionately, "She has put on weight." Two months later she was found in the garden rolling on the ground in pain and she was rushed to the hospital. Two days later, she gave birth to a premature seven-and-a-half-month-old baby girl.

The NGOs and women's groups went on a rampage at once. A woman staying in the outhouse of a supreme court judge had given birth to an illegitimate child. More importantly, a mute, mentally challenged woman had been raped. The culprit could not be allowed to get away. There were hundreds of people who visited my house.

Nandita went to the short-stay home twice a week. Who knew when it had happened? She had not complained to anyone. Although, being mute and mentally challenged, no one knew how she could have complained.

One day as I entered our house, I asked Shyamlee, "The photograph on the mantelpiece in the drawing room is missing; where is it?"

She did not say anything. After some probing I learnt that it had been taken away from our house. The NGOs had coaxed Nandita to divulge the name of the culprit and when they had taken the photograph from our house and asked her to identify the culprit she had pointed towards me.

That was it. Nandita's identification made headline news in the newspaper. "Woman claims supreme court judge is the father!" The journalists had a field day. The law is the same for men and women, proclaimed the press. No one is above law. Lawmakers cannot become lawbreakers. The newspapers made the most of it.

Shyamlee began to treat me as though I was a god with feet of clay. One day was all it took to transform me from an upright judge to a downright criminal. It was a long trial by the media.

And then I did the unthinkable. I offered to undergo a DNA test to disprove paternity and offered to resign and face criminal charges if I was proved the culprit. I took the wind out of the sails of the raging NGOs. From being the culprit I became the martyr.

The results of the DNA test took a long time to come.

"Thank God Kartik is not here," murmured Shyamlee. "I don't know how he would have faced it."

Kartik had been packed off to the USA in September, much before the scandal made the headlines. For years he had been pleading to go to the USA to study but I had steadily refused. At last I had capitulated.

"Mom, just chill," butted in Vidya, who was my staunch supporter. "Nandita is not a saint. Everyone knows that although she is not married she has a child who lives in the short-stay home. She may be mute and mentally challenged but she could have made a noise. She would have had scratch marks over her body, she would gesticulate. This was a case of consensual sex."

I blanched on hearing Vidya's words. How could she discuss this so candidly before her parents? Perhaps I had lost touch with today's generation.

"It could have been just anyone," surmised Vidya. "The chowkidar at the gate, or the *doodhwala*, the postman, the gardener, the pizza delivery boy, or any of the people who had access to the house. Just anyone. We do not even know it happened here. It could have happened in the short-stay home."

"Then why did she point to his photo?" cried Shyamlee. And for once I could hear the pain in her voice.

"Wishful thinking, perhaps!" grinned Vidya wickedly. "Maybe she dreams of being in your shoes."

Shyamlee shrugged and walked away from the room. The role of an aggrieved wife was new to her. For too long she had played the role of the fallen woman.

The DNA test had proved that I was not the father of Nandita's child. The media went overboard in trying to restore my image. But the damage was done. I resigned from my post soon after. No one could understand why I had resigned after the DNA test result had cleared me.

"Why are you resigning?" asked Shyamlee. Was it a sense of guilt that was making her ask this question, I wondered caustically, or was it the loss of perks?

"Why, Dad, why?" Vidya said in bewilderment.

I knew the answer, but I couldn't disclose it to anyone. I knew what no one else knew. I knew that many months ago, one night, when I had gone out to the terrace for a breath of fresh air, I had seen a figure slink out of the outhouse and enter the main house. It had disappeared into the shadows. I had heard a door open and then close. Then the lights in the room at the end of the corridor had come on. It was Kartik's room.

I thought of the photograph the head of the NGO SATYA had taken away with her. It was a family photo of Vidya, Shyamlee, Kartik and me. Nandita's shaking finger had pointed to Kartik. The NGOs and the activists had seen what they had wanted to. But I had said nothing in my defence. I knew better than anyone else what the punishment for rape was. And even if it had been consensual sex and not rape, it would have been impossible for Kartik to prove it. I could not let my son's life be ruined because, like his mother, he could not resist temptation.

The truth was that I had not capitulated to his request to study abroad; I had forced Kartik to go abroad for his graduation, even though I had to dip into my life's savings to fund his education.

But I do have a conscience. As a judge it was my duty to dispense justice. But since I had failed to provide justice to Nandita, I knew I had to pay the price.

# The Unforgiven

Manya sat on the wooden *jhoola* in the verandah, rocking herself, pushing the swing higher and higher with her feet, oblivious of any premonition of disaster.

When the landline rang, she assumed that it was a business call for her father. Even when she saw his face turning chalk-white, his lips moving soundlessly as he gripped the receiver tightly, she did not guess that the news concerned her. Then she saw him knock his favourite flower vase in a hurry. Without even giving it a glance, he reached her and said, "Manya, my child, it's Mohit. He has been wounded."

Wounded. The words reverberated in her head. Was Mohit wounded or was he dead? Images of Mohit flashed before her eyes.

So engrossed was she in her thoughts that she did not hear her mother enter the verandah. "Have faith in God, Manya," she said, her hand on Manya's shoulder. "Everything will be alright."

"Don't," Manya said brusquely, brushing aside her mother's hand in anger. If God could ensure everything to be alright, then thousands of women would not become war widows, lakhs of children would not be orphaned, thousands of soldiers would not be killed, and lakhs of them would not lose their limbs, during every war.

Manya gave a cry of distress, ran across to her bedroom and locked the door from inside. Mohit's picture stood on her dressing table. Captain Mohit Varma of the Gorkha Regiment looked dashing in uniform. She looked at the photograph, pulled open a drawer, took out a diamond ring and slipped it onto her finger.

"Manya. Manya." The knock on her door became insistent. Manya opened it and found her father standing outside. He gave her a tentative smile and said, "Mohit is being flown down to Delhi tomorrow."

After he had left the room Manya knelt on the floor and began to sob. Afterwards she returned to the drawing room and heard her mother say, "Manya has taken this very hard. We don't even know how badly Mohit is injured. I am a little worried. I think that she wasn't very happy with the engagement. I am afraid that we have rushed her into it."

"You are only saying all this because when Mohit's leave was cancelled and he was called to Kashmir, he left for Kargil without seeing her," her father said gruffly. "But that doesn't mean anything. Manya and Mohit have known each other for years. They grew up together."

Manya rushed out of the room blindly. Yes, her father was right—Mohit and she knew each other well. They had played on these very lawns, with Mohit lifting his Leo Mattel toy gun and firing rapidly at her, or tying her up with ropes and making her a prisoner of war. But that was not reason enough to get married. She should have rejected the proposal when it came. But when Mohit's father had said, "Mohit won the Sword of Honour in Khadakwasla and was declared the best cadet," and her father had beamed with delight, she had found it impossible to say no.

A day before the engagement Mohit and she had a long talk about the future.

"You may not be able to pursue a high-profile career. Army officers are always on the move, and I would like to have my wife with me," he had said and she had smiled.

"You look sombre," she had said quietly, as she saw him turn serious.

"It's nothing." He had shaken his head and a lock of hair had fallen on his forehead. Why was his hair not cut in the typical crew cut? "You do realise that an army man can go to war at any time," he had muttered.

His words had shocked her. The war that had appeared to be a remote danger had become a distinct possibility. She thought of the Chinese aggression in 1962. It had happened long before she was born. But her parents, who had been children at that time, still talked about it. Her mother spoke of the air-raid sirens that blew in the middle of the night, making all the members of her joint family scramble out of their warm beds and silken quilts or Raymond blankets into the spiral staircase between the ground and the first floor.

"It was sturdy in there; even during a bomb blast it would survive," said her mother.

Manya had heard her dad speak of how black paper was put on the windows and ventilators to prevent light seeping out of the house at the time the air-raid sirens blew. She had heard of the India–Pakistan war in 1965 and of Bangladesh's War of Liberation in 1971. Her grand-uncle talked about it on dark wintry nights, telling her tales of his stay in Bangladesh and narrating his role in escorting the Pakistani General Niazi to Jabalpur Jail after the Pakistani Army had surrendered in Dhaka.

But this was different. It was for real. And it affected her. But now it was too late to back out.

The next morning, she learnt that Mohit had been admitted to the Army Hospital in the Delhi Cantonment. Her parents decided to visit him that evening. When she entered the drawing room in the afternoon, she found her father on the phone. He looked at her pityingly and then looked away and she had a curious sense of foreboding.

"We cannot go to the hospital today," her father mumbled. "Mohit needs an emergency operation."

"What kind of an operation?" Manya persisted.

"I do not know," he said gruffly and walked away.

"You are hiding something from me, aren't you?" she asked her mother, who was busy looking at the floor. "Tell me, Mom," Manya demanded. "What are you hiding from me?"

Her mother looked up, and then held her tight before saying, "Manya. Gangrene has set in Mohit's leg. They have no choice but to amputate it."

Manya closed her eyes to stop the tears that sprang up. Maybe this was just a bad dream that would go away. Maybe if she just blinked hard it would disappear. Maybe she would wake up and the nightmare would be over.

"Manya," said her father, putting his finger under her chin and raising her head, "look at me."

Seeing the concern on his face, she began sobbing.

"Here," said her dad, pulling out his plaid handkerchief, "take it."

She wiped her tears, shamed by her weakness. She knew Mohit would want her to be strong for his sake.

"Listen," said her dad, "this is not a marriage; it is just an engagement, and engagements can be broken."

"Why?" asked Manya.

He was taken aback. "Because Mohit has lost a leg."

"What if he had lost it after our marriage?" she countered, leaving him speechless.

The next morning Manya decided to meet Mohit on her own. She met Mohit's parents at the reception in the Army Hospital. They seemed to have aged overnight. Mrs Varma's hair had greyed and her face was completely ravaged. The skin around her chin hung loose and her eyes looked glazed. General Varma's shoulders were stooped as though he was Atlas, carrying the world on his shoulders. Manya stood helplessly at a corner.

"It is now up to you to cheer him up," said General Varma. "Mohit is a little depressed."

"A little" was an understatement, Manya realised when the nurse called out her name and escorted her to Mohit's room. Mohit seemed to have shrunk. His cheeks were gaunt and his eyes unseeing. He did not even turn his head when she entered but continued to gaze at the wall in front of him as though he could read his future in the shadows across it.

Manya stood silently, waiting for him to look at her. Then she cleared her throat.

The nurse who entered the room said, "Mohit, you have a visitor."

"Who is it?" he asked gruffly, turning his head. "Manya," he said formally on seeing her, "please sit down." His glance seemed to pierce through her.

"Did Mohit receive my letter?" Manya wondered, her heart thumping. The words that she had written to him were imprinted in her mind, as though someone had taken a chisel and carved them into stone.

"Dear Mohit," she had written, "I am writing to you for a favour. I want a release from this engagement. I want my freedom back. No. There is no other man in my life. I want to be freed simply because I am not cut out to be a soldier's wife. I cannot spend day after day waiting for news of you from the front. I cannot see you going to war with a smile on my face, not knowing when you would return or if you would return at all. I am not cut out for heroics. I have simple dreams, of a home, a husband and children. I cannot lose myself in huge rambling army bungalows, while waiting in dread for the phone to ring with a disembodied voice telling me, 'Madam, I am sorry to inform you that Mohit Varma is no more.' I hate the thought of being a widow, and even if you live to be a hundred years I would die a little every time you were at war, wondering if a landmine, an enemy bullet or a terrorist attack would end your life. I know many women have lived this kind of life. Your mother did it for years. But this life is not for me. So give me back the freedom I ask for."

She had written the letter a fortnight after the engagement, the fear of an imminent war preying upon her mind; she was afraid that she would lose her courage if she waited any longer.

That very day the news of the Kargil War had broken out. A day later Mohit, who was at home on annual leave, had been posted to Kargil.

"Too bad he didn't have time to wish you goodbye," her mother said, while Manya wondered what madness had made her write what she did. She wondered if the letter had reached him and hoped that it had not. She went to Mohit's house a week later.

While she was rummaging through his cupboard his mother entered his room. "Are you looking for something?" she asked Manya pointedly, and all Manya could do was mumble, "No, I was just missing him."

As soon as she said this she realised that it was true: the fact was that she was missing Mohit, missing him so terribly that it was almost a physical ache.

Standing in the hospital room, Manya knew that she should have felt vindicated; her worst nightmare had almost come true. Instead she felt hollow. "Mohit," she asked, "how are you?"

"How do you expect a one-legged soldier to be?" he asked unsmilingly. His face was pale and drawn.

"This is not the Mohit I knew," she said lightly.

"The Mohit you knew was able-bodied, with the world at his feet. The Mohit before you is an amputee," he retorted.

She blanched on hearing his words. She could not see his amputated leg. His legs were covered. She had not realised until then that the operation had destroyed not just Mohit's leg but much more. She remembered Mohit's father's words: "It is now up to you."

"It's not the end of the world," she murmured.

"For an infantryman without a leg, it is," Mohit said.

"Captain Pankaj Joshi lost both legs," she retorted, "yet he rose to be a lieutenant general."

"You seem to have done research on the subject," Mohit said sardonically. She flushed on hearing his words.

Manya left Mohit's room emotionally worn out and battle-scarred. She knew that the months ahead were going to be difficult. She was not sure she would be able to endure them. Her first instinct was to flee.

"How long can you do that?" she said to herself, squaring her shoulders. "What you did was unforgivable."

She guessed from Mohit's remarks that he had received her letter and he was furious with her. That was evident from his behaviour. But he knew, as she did, that he needed her.

"I will make it up to Mohit," she promised herself, "even if it takes me a lifetime to do it.

"Was it my letter that had made him courageous and even a little foolhardy?" Manya wondered guiltily. "Did he climb to the picket, unmindful of the sound of gunfire from across the border because he had become oblivious to fear, consumed as he was by a towering rage towards a girl who did not have the courage to face life with him? Am I responsible for Mohit's unfortunate condition?"

Manya returned to the reception and once again met Mohit's mother, who seemed completely shattered. This is what happens when you have just one child, who becomes the centre of your universe, she thought. She decided that Mohit and she would have at least two children. She walked up to Mohit's mother, put her hands on her shoulder and pressed it gently with her fingers. "Aunty," Manya urged, "we have to be brave, for Mohit's sake."

Geeta Varma looked away. She knew that if she tried to speak she would break down completely.

"I will see you off, Manya," said Mohit's father as he walked with her towards the gate.

Geeta Varma looked at their retreating backs in silence. For how many months had she hated Manya? She could no longer remember. It was ever since the letter had arrived, on the very day that Mohit was to leave for Kargil.

What instinct had made her pick up the letter? Was it a premonition or just sheer curiosity? She did not know. But she was happy she had read it. Had the letter reached Mohit she was sure she would not have got her wounded son back. She would have got back his body wrapped in the national flag, like a war hero.

She remembered the times when she had stood by the door of her house, gazing outside unseeingly, or sat by the window, drumming her fingers on the window sill, tension rife within her. Yet she had never written anything to her husband. She had never voiced her fears to him, but Manya had voiced hers to Mohit.

She was glad Mohit did not know about the letter. He would never forgive Manya if he did. But Mohit needed Manya right now. She was glad that Manya would never have the courage to ask Mohit outright about the letter. She would look after Mohit, whether out of love or guilt, it didn't matter. And Mohit, who loved her completely, would eventually heal in her company.

Geeta Varma took the letter out of an ivory box, read the words scribbled on it with wet eyes and then returned it to the box. This was one secret, she promised to herself, which she would carry with herself to her grave.

# The Untruth

The modern security lock is the best thing to be invented after sliced bread. It can lock the door from outside as well as inside. It takes away the entire tension from waiting. I can now sleep peacefully instead of waiting half the night, my ear cocked towards the door to hear the sound of a car entering through the gate, the screeching of the tyres, the sound of unsteady feet staggering up to the door and the peal of the doorbell. I no longer have to see Leena tumble out of bed to open the door for Rohan, and watch her return to our bedroom, her silence echoing her concern and disappointment. With the modern security lock in place, I can go to bed knowing that I can sleep undisturbed by my adolescent son's late nights.

That night I had no cause for worry as Leena was accompanying Rohan to the party. Leena's colleagues were Rohan's best friend's parents. I knew my son was in safe hands.

I woke up at the crack of dawn and was tempted to pull the bedcover over my head and go back to sleep. But I needed to do my five-kilometre walk. Those were the doctor's orders and Leena, my guardian angel, ensured that, come rain or thunder, I would abide by them.

The bed beside me was empty; I guessed that the ever-considerate Leena had slept in the guest room to ensure that I did not wake up in the middle of the night.

I grimaced some more. Leena was the picture-perfect wife. Before her I appeared to be an unkempt slob. Then I smiled guiltily. Leena was the best thing that had ever happened to me, even better than the modern lock and sliced bread, I thought flippantly.

I whistled as I wore my Nike tee shirt and grey shorts, shoved my feet into Nike shoes after failing to find a single pair of matching socks, and left for my walk. I limped slightly as I walked towards Lodhi Gardens, the spur on my foot playing up once again. Age-related health problems, I rued. I was no longer a young 25-year-old. I was touching 50.

As I walked towards Lodhi Gardens, I breathed deeply—my own improvisation of pranayama. Once I had reached my destination, I entered the right gate and began walking briskly before breaking into a run. I imagined the three Lodhi kings, Balhol Lodhi, Sikander Lodhi and Ibrahim Lodhi, step out of the pages of history onto these lawns.

I decided to break my stride, abandon the beaten jogger's track and turn towards the stream, in the midst of which stood a fountain that squirted a jet of water that sparkled like a profusion of jewels in the sunlight. Ducks glided on the algae-ridden water, white specks dancing on their brown and black bodies. Pink and white lotus blossoms floated in the water. I sat on a bench by the fountain, mesmerised as always by the scene before me, and wondered where Leena and I had gone wrong. A senior bank officer of the Reserve Bank of India and a chartered accountant with his own firm had sired an only son who was on his way to becoming a school dropout. Rohan had been a docile mama's boy before reaching adolescence. There was no defining moment when the change had occurred. Perhaps we had been so caught up with our careers that we had not seen the indications of change, not understood that his sullen disposition was not merely a sign of awkward adolescence but something else. We had not realised that he had begun experimenting with drugs, that the half-opened bottle of whisky in our glass cabinet had become lighter in colour because Rohan had diluted it with water, and that the matchboxes that kept disappearing from the kitchen were helping to light Rohan's cigarettes. We failed to check the company he was keeping and didn't realise that his friends would only take him downhill.

The rebellion simmering within Rohan became a revolt when he refused to opt for Science, against Leena's wishes, and when he began to fail with unfailing regularity once her will prevailed. The breach was complete when he fell from the balcony, fracturing his leg, and lay in bed for two months, virtually having to learn to walk again, first with crutches and then unaided. The fracture left him with no limp, but effectively put an end to his cricketing career. I had a terrible showdown with Rohan when I defended Leena, whom Rohan for some reason blamed for the accident. He had shouted, "There is no point in talking; you always have blinkers on your eyes."

He now had only one passion, his guitar, and the music that emanated from his room often threatened to shatter my peace and equanimity, not to mention my eardrums.

I shook my head, trying to shrug off the depression that had begun to engulf me. As I got up I realised that I had disturbed a flock of parrots, pecking bajra on the grass. Some of them flew up and sat on the branches of the *gulmohar* tree while others took flight and zigzagged across the sky, like a streak of lightning, boosting my spirits instantly. I began walking briskly, ignoring the laughter emanating from the laughter club, unnerving in its shrillness. I stopped for a few minutes to marvel at the suppleness of the human body and the perseverance of men and women who forced their bodies into amazing contortions while doing yoga. I remembered the times Leena and I spent in Lodhi Gardens, secretly holding hands when we thought no one was looking. That had been 25 years ago. We had spent the intervening years trying to adjust to each other. I tried to live up to Leena's exalted standards, while she in turn learnt to live with my imperfections. Rohan, our only son, arrived eight years after marriage, and we considered him a cherished gift from God.

I thought of our 25th wedding anniversary, which was still a fortnight away. I would have preferred a quiet dinner for two, but Leena wanted the whole world to share our big day. I smiled silently as I headed back to my house in Golf Links, which my dadaji had built, and stood admiring it for a few minutes before turning the key and entering.

"Hi," I heard the lilt in Leena's voice as I entered the drawing room. She was standing at the kitchen counter. Entering the kitchen, I saw her deftly beat up eggs in a glass bowl, add sugar, flour and milk and beat it lightly once again.

"What's for breakfast?" I asked casually, only for her to confirm what I had already guessed.

"Pancakes," she said cheerfully.

I made a face once her back was turned. Pancakes had been our staple Sunday breakfast ever since Leena had returned from Europe six months ago, totally enamoured by the continental breakfasts, including pancakes, maple syrup, clotted cream and strawberry jam. I did not have the heart to tell her that pancakes with maple syrup were as big a caloric bomb as aloo parathas, which she had banned as I was a borderline diabetic.

"Where is Rohan?" I asked, my voice neutral. I was sure he was still asleep and would get up only in time for what Leena euphemistically called "Sunday brunch."

"He has gone out," she said.

My spirits lifted on hearing her. "Jogging," I said aloud, although Leena seemed not to have heard me.

"When did you get back last night?" I asked, pulling a stool and watching her cook, not betraying the anxiety I felt.

"Late," said Leena, her mind on more important things, like flipping the pancake in the non-stick pan. "I didn't want to disturb you."

The doorbell rang just when Leena had begun to spread another pancake on the pan. I opened the door since the servants had taken the Sunday off and Leena's hands were smeared with flour.

Two policemen stood at the doorstep. One was tall, dark and saturnine. The other one was short and stocky with a Hitler-like moustache. The Hitler lookalike with his greying sideburns was obviously older.

I panicked. This was my worst nightmare come true. "Is it Rohan? Has he met with an accident?" I shouted.

I saw the look of surprise on their faces and realised that this was not about Rohan. Relief swept all over me. Thank God Rohan was alright. When life is at stake, everything else fades into nothingness, disagreements, children's insolence, board marks. Life takes precedence over everything else.

"Is the black Honda City, number DL 5C 2552, yours?" the older policeman asked.

"Yes," I said, "what's wrong?"

"The car mowed down three people on the sidewalk last night. All three are dead." The implications of the statement were horrific.

"May we see your car?" asked the policeman.

"It's in our garage," I said.

"It's in the workshop," Leena corrected me. "Rohan has gone to drop it off."

"How can it be in the workshop?" I asked. "Did you have an accident?" I realised that it was the wrong question to have asked.

"It's just a dent," said Leena quickly. "I thought I should attend to it immediately."

I was shocked. To which workshop had she sent it?

I got my answer a moment later when Rohan came striding through the door. His face turned pale as he saw the police. Guilt seemed to be writ large on it.

"Officers, please speak to me." Leena was brusque and businesslike. She did not appear to be intimidated by them, unlike me. She had not become the general manager of the Reserve Bank of India just like that.

"Madam, your car was on the road at that time," said the Hitler lookalike.

"How do you know that?" she countered, unaware of the irony of her turning the tables on them and becoming the interrogator.

"It was caught on the security camera, Madam. It had been speeding."

She shrugged once again. "It doesn't mean it caused the accident," she said with a confidence that was astonishing.

"We have a witness," the policeman said.

"I thought you said that the three men had been mowed down," Leena retorted.

"We got an anonymous phone call," he admitted.

That had her stumped.

"Who was driving the car?" the policeman asked her.

"I was driving," she said bravely.

I looked at her admiringly. Leena was a lioness protecting her cub. There was nothing as strong as maternal love. Leena may not have been the most demonstrative of mothers, but she would not feed Rohan to the wolves, come what may. Rohan was safe with her.

"I was driving," she asserted. "I had gone with him to the party and was driving when we returned."

"Are you sure, Madam?" asked the policeman, seeing Rohan's pale face. "Are you sure it was not your son who was driving?"

"Of course not," said Leena quickly. "He is not yet 18."

"How old is he?" asked the policeman.

"He is 17," Leena said.

"Does he have a learner's license for a motorcycle?" he asked.

"Yes," interjected Rohan.

We did not see any need for telling the policemen that he had been driving a car since he was 14. It was illegal, of course, but I prided myself on the fact that it was I who had taught him to drive.

"Who is the owner of the car?" asked the policeman.

"I am." Rohan's admission came after a long pause.

It was my birthday gift to him on his 17th birthday, a peace offering to heal the breach between us. The car was presented with the rider that Rohan would only drive when one of his parents was present.

The policemen looked at Rohan's six-foot two-inch frame appraisingly and Hitler said, "Honda City is a big car; I think you were driving it."

"Officer, I was driving," Rohan's admission came as a shock both to the policemen and to me. Only Leena was not surprised. She knew the truth, of course.

"We need to take your son for questioning," said the policeman, as pompous as Hitler must have been.

"Why?" I asked.

"He is old enough to drive and to kill, surely he is old enough to answer our questions?" said the policeman.

"Officer, he is only 17," I said, and asked Rohan to get his learner's license as proof of his age—but Rohan returned empty-handed.

"Oh no, Rohan, not again," groaned Leena while Rohan smiled sheepishly. He had misplaced his learner's license yet again.

The policemen had no warrant of arrest but Rohan volunteered to go with them.

"Don't go, Rohan," I urged.

He turned back and gave me an enigmatic smile before climbing into the police van.

"He needs a lawyer," said Leena once the police had left. "One who can get him released on bail."

"It is a Sunday, but let me find out," I promised.

"My poor son; behind the bravado he must be petrified," said Leena.

I sat down on the sofa and began to weep. Then I felt a gentle touch on my shoulder. It was Leena.

"It's alright," she consoled, "he is just 17. They cannot try him or send him to jail. He will be let off on probation or at worst be convicted and be sent to a juvenile home for a year."

"What sort of life will he have after this?" I asked her in a shaking voice.

"What kind of life does he have, anyway?" asked Leena.

I looked up hearing the bitterness and scorn in her voice. Rohan had been a disappointment to both Leena and me. Leena, who planned everything in life, had mapped out Rohan's career, with a B.Tech from IIT Kanpur and an MBA from IIM Ahmedabad, followed by a career in investment banking. But when Rohan began spending all his time either on the sports field or in his rock band, and had transformed into a sullen defiant teenager who experimented with drinks, drugs and cigarettes, all before he was 16, Leena was heartbroken.

"Rohan is a school dropout, with a compartment in Maths. He cannot get admission in any good college this year, anyway. So how does the probation matter? He is not planning to join government service."

"What happened last night?" I asked.

"Pretty much what the policeman said," explained Leena. "Rohan was driving. I had not seen him drinking, but perhaps he had disguised the drinks in the glasses of Coke he was downing. Had I known this, I would have refused to let him drive. You know he is a careful driver, but he lost control of the car when a dog came from nowhere and ran across the road. In a bid to save it, Rohan drove on the sidewalk and ran over the three men."

"Why didn't he stop?" I wondered aloud.

"He was scared. Frankly, I too was scared. I didn't try to stop him, so I am guilty, too. When we reached home at around 1 am we saw the dent on the car. I told Rohan to take it to the workshop in the morning. I was trying to protect him. I had hoped that the police would not be able to track down the car."

I looked at Leena in amazement, wondering whether to admire her for going to such lengths to protect Rohan or to castigate her for not going to the police.

"Three men have died," I said, unable to get over this nightmare. "Do you realise that Rohan is guilty of murder?"

"No, Pranav," she said immediately, "he is guilty of rash and negligent driving."

"He should not have been driving after drinking," I shouted. "What if the police had stopped him for a breath analyser test? Then he would have been guilty of not just rash and negligent driving but of drunken driving as well. He is not 18 yet. He is not permitted to drive. His driving a car is a crime and as parents we are guilty as well." I was shocked by the fact that Leena had been so uncaring about the men Rohan had mowed down. "You should have been driving," I screamed.

"Pranav, you know I am a hopeless driver," admitted Leena, shrugging her shoulder helplessly.

I knew that. I had witnessed this for myself. Once I had seen Leena panic-stricken, in fact almost paralysed, when she had seen a truck bearing down on her. But for Rohan's presence of mind that had made him grab the wheel, we would all have been dead. Actually, I admitted to myself, I should have accompanied them to the party, but I had begged off with the excuse that my back was playing up. The truth was that parties bored me. Inane conversation, forced laughter, catty gossip and mild flirtations—I could not handle any of this. Much to Leena's disappointment, she had realised that I was a social disaster.

"Are we fighting?" Leena asked suddenly.

"No, we are not," I said apologetically.

We seldom fought. We had mild disagreements at most. Today for the first time in years I had shouted at her. But the circumstances were extenuating. Then I thought of Rohan and the way he had looked at me while leaving. I had not been able to fathom the expression on his face.

"I am going to the police station to meet Rohan," I said.

I drove my Volkswagen Vento into the police station. Rohan was sitting on a bench with his head down, not inside the police lockup—thank God.

"Rohan," I called out loudly. He looked up and saw me. The look in his eyes was a mixture of open derision, contempt and scorn.

Suddenly I understood. "You weren't driving," I hazarded a guess. "You are doing all this for your mother."

Everything began to fall into place. Leena's pretence to take the rap on Rohan's behalf. Her acquiescence when the police zeroed in on him.

"You were drunk," I surmised shrewdly, "and so Leena was driving."

"And we all know how she drives," said Rohan and began to laugh.

The car must have zigzagged, but Leena had to drive because Rohan had downed too many drinks. Trying to save the dog, she must have driven onto the pavement and over the three sleeping pavement dwellers. Having mowed them down, she must have continued to drive recklessly, deaf to Rohan's entreaties to slow down, to return and seek medical aid for the victims. With her characteristic nerves of steel, Leena must have told Rohan to wash the car and take it to the workshop the next morning. This morning, with ice in her veins, she was busy flipping pancakes, hoping to get away with murder.

"Aw, Dad," said Rohan awkwardly, patting my shoulder. "She cannot own up to the accident. She has too much to lose, her promotion that is due in two weeks and the course she has been selected for in Harvard next month. She cannot go to jail."

"What about you?" I asked.

"I will be on probation or in a juvenile home for a while. Anyway, I was not planning to take on a government job. So many celebrities have had accidents and nothing has ever happened to them. I may be able to get away with it."

Words of wisdom from a 17-year-old or the borrowed logic of his mother, who had managed to brainwash him somehow? "Why didn't you stop to take them to the hospital?" I reprimanded him.

"I wanted to," Rohan said, "but..."

I could easily fill in the blanks. His mother would not have stopped.

Something else struck me then. "Were you the one who called the police?" I asked.

"Yes, I was," he admitted. "I wanted the police to take them to the hospital in case they had any hope of survival."

My heart swelled with pride. My son had far more humanity and compassion than his mother.

Dropout, failure, loser, Leena could call Rohan whatever she wanted, but in my eyes Rohan was a fine young man. I hugged him and said, "I am proud of you and I will make sure that nothing happens to you."

I remembered that three eminent criminal lawyers were my clients. The time had come to call in some favours. But before that I had some unfinished business to attend to. On the way back I wondered about Rohan's fall from the balcony, which had brought such a cataclysmic change in him. Was it Leena who had pushed him in anger, instead of trying to save him from falling, as she had claimed? Was that the reason why Rohan had turned more aggressive and recalcitrant?

When I returned home I found Leena sitting in the drawing room switching channels on our new Samsung LED TV. What had I expected her to do—collapse on the bed in grief?

"So how is Rohan?" she asked, her voice just the right blend of concern and tenderness.

"All grown up," I claimed, my voice curt.

She looked up then. My words sounded almost like a compliment. Leena was used to my abusing Rohan. "I know," I said quietly. My words were innocuous. I did not say, "I know the truth."

But Leena understood immediately. "Did Rohan say something?" she asked anxiously.

"I am speaking of everything he didn't say," I murmured.

"Rohan is responsible," she insisted aggressively. "Had he not been drunk, he would have been driving. Then the accident would never have happened, and in case it did, he would have actually been responsible."

"Why, Leena, why?" I asked.

She knew what I was asking her. Why did she make Rohan the scapegoat? Why didn't she have enough courage to take responsibility for her actions?

"My promotion to the post of chief general manager is due in two weeks' time," she said. "I cannot afford to go to jail. Rohan is not an adult yet. Besides, he is a school dropout."

"Not a dropout," I cut in. "He had a compartment in Maths. I am sure he will clear it soon."

"No court will convict him," argued Leena, "but in case I am arrested, I will go to jail." Clearly Leena was remembering the Sanjeev Nanda case, wherein he had mowed down four pavement dwellers and had to spend years in jail.

I began to clap loudly. I had never seen this facet of Leena. I also experienced a sense of déjà vu. I had heard these arguments from Rohan just half an hour ago. I had no desire to get into a harangue with her. I knew that as always

I would emerge vanquished. Instead I picked up the strolley bag in the guest room, which Leena always kept packed for my unexpected tours, and began walking out of the door.

"Look, Pranav," she pleaded, her equanimity shattered at last, "believe me, Rohan will be back soon."

"After spending a year or more in a juvenile home for something he didn't do?" I said. "After carrying the tag of being a killer at the age of 17 for the rest of his life?"

Leena continued to argue. "You cannot throw away 25 years of our marriage because of one accident. Our 25th wedding anniversary is due in a fortnight. Everyone is coming for the celebration, even the governor of RBI. What will they say?"

I still did not say anything.

"You cannot walk away like this. You cannot go to the police and tell the truth. What will happen to me?"

I looked at her then. All I could see was concern for herself. Then I recalled the stricken look on Rohan's face. I knew what I had to do, even if it cost me my marriage and Leena her freedom.

"What about Rohan?" I asked her once again, making one last-ditch effort to awaken her conscience.

"Believe me, he will be back," her voice floated towards me confidently once again.

"But I won't," I said, before stepping out.

# If the Truth be Told

"So you have decided to move on. Well, seven years is a long time to wait for someone."

The words, spoken casually, cause a minor explosion in the hall. Everyone is utterly stunned that the memories of the past, which I have tried so hard to forget, have been raked up so mercilessly.

"It is the law of the land," I say stiffly. "Section 108 of the Indian Evidence Act 1896 says that a man shall be presumed dead if nothing is heard of him for seven years."

"I know," acknowledges Justice Rajat Desai satirically. I realise that somehow he holds me responsible for the fact that Amit had walked out of our house one day after our marriage, simply because his ex-girlfriend had committed suicide on our wedding day.

"So the mourning period is over," Suhana starts where Justice Desai had left, but she hisses out the words, a cobra just out of hibernation.

If she had her way, I would spend my entire life in the twilight zone between hope and despair. I think of the visits to the city hospital, the morgue and the police station, looking for Amit, and recall the advertisements in the newspapers and the announcements over the radio and television. A grown man could simply not vanish into thin air. Amit seemed to have done just that.

I know that Suhana wants me to live my life in suspended animation, cling to hope, run with flying feet every time the doorbell rings, hoping that there will be news of Amit. Suhana wants my eyes to light up at the sight of every letter, in case it is Amit's missive about his whereabouts.

I cannot tell her that hope within me had died long ago, and had given way to fear. Every time I see a police officer I am afraid that he is the harbinger of bad news. Every time I read about an unidentified body I dread that it is Amit's.

Was he the victim of an accident? Had he become amnesic? Or had he renounced the world and sought refuge amongst the sages in the Himalayas? Was he a saffron-robed mendicant in Badrinath or had he ended as an unclaimed body on a medical student's dissection table? Seven years is a long time to let imagination run riot. It is not only a long time to wait for someone; it is also a long time to mourn the loss of a loved one. The time has come to pick up the pieces and move on.

"There is evil in the air," asserts my friend Rubina, sniffing around like a bloodhound. She is a tarot-card reader and is sensitive to the atmosphere.

I quiver. Misfortune has been pursuing me for seven years. I could do with a dose of good luck.

Rajesh's appearance on the scene soothes my nerves. He looks at me adoringly, with dog-like devotion. He has trailed me for years. He cannot believe he is getting me after all. I wonder at fate, which had created a strange quartet. Rajesh wanted me, I wanted Amit, and Amit wanted Ayesha. And Ayesha was a delusional, crazy, hallucinating girl, who could not distinguish between reality and make-believe, who eyed everyone with suspicion.

I slip my hand into Rajesh's. The engagement is merely a formality; we are already a couple.

The engagement ceremony begins. Rajesh puts a diamond solitaire ring on my finger. As I begin to slip a ring on his finger a voice booms out, "Couldn't you even wait for seven years to be over?"

I spin around immediately. I can never forget the voice; it could melt my bones, as could his touch. I begin to sway and Rajesh lifts me and carries me to the sofa.

When I gain consciousness, I see Rajesh hovering over me. His face looks pinched. He too recognises the voice, and how could he not? Rajesh, Amit and I had grown up together. We were childhood friends; Ayesha was an outsider. It was understood by everyone, I reminisce, that Amit and I would get married someday. But everything changed after Ayesha had come along.

I get up with a jerk. Who is the owner of the voice? I find that all eyes are riveted upon a man in white kurta-pyjamas with a long flowing beard and shoulder-length hair. Nothing much is visible about his face except his eyes. But his eyes are different. Not Amit's. Certainly not Amit's. He is an imposter, a mimic, someone who has learnt to imitate Amit's voice.

"An imposter," my voice rings out confidently. "There was a similar case during British times..." I am a practitioner of law but I begin to falter as the name escapes me.

"The Bhawal Sanyasi case. The case of Ramendra Narayan Roy, the second brother among the Kumars of the Bhawal Estate, who died on 7 May 1907 and was cremated in Darjeeling. But a hailstorm interrupted his cremation and later the body disappeared. In 1921, he reappeared in Dhaka, where his wife called him an imposter; but the case, which went right up to the privy council, was won by him."

All eyes are on the man in the white kurta-pyjamas, who had displayed his extensive knowledge of law. He is not a swami, despite his clothes. But is he Amit?

"No need for forensics as in the case of Bhawal Sanyasi, or DNA testing," he shrugs. "Give me half an hour and I can prove my identity."

How? I wonder: does he have documentary evidence?

"No," says Dad, "you are not going anywhere."

I suppose he does not want to face a repeat of what had happened seven years ago, and is afraid that the man in white may pull a Houdini. I know what Dad had in mind when he handed over the man to my sister Ananya, who runs a beauty parlour.

For half an hour, I sit amidst a babble of sounds, my eyes closed, and pray. I do not know what I am praying for. The return of Amit, whose very presence made my pulse beat faster, and who had left his wife of one day because his girlfriend of two years had committed suicide on the day of his wedding? Or the exposure of an imposter so that I can begin to live once again, this time with Rajesh, who has stood staunchly by me for seven years?

Half an hour later he returns, his hair cut and shampooed, his face clean-shaven, displaying his baby-soft skin, his eyes unfathomable. Amit! Unmistakably Amit. My breath is ragged. Amit always had this effect on me. I am a somnambulist who has suddenly been cured of sleepwalking, I am an accident victim who has woken up miraculously after being in a coma for seven years.

"Young man," questions Dad, unable to disguise his fondness for Amit despite everything, "why did you disappear?"

"Because Ayesha committed suicide."

Amit's words, spoken baldly, are a slap on my face.

"You left Nandini for that demented Ayesha. No one ever knew when she was lying and when she was telling the truth. She accused her classmates of rape and then withdrew the accusation when she was advised to undergo a medical examination? And then she became pregnant mysteriously. She was a girl of doubtful morals, who did not herself know how to distinguish between the truth and lies," says Dad.

Amit's eyes lock onto mine. I see the half-quizzical, half-censorious look in them. I have betrayed a dead girl's confidence. "Well, now that she is dead..." I begin lamely.

Amit may not have wanted Ayesha's memories to be tarnished, but I cannot forgive her for choosing to die on my wedding day and ensuring that Amit belonged to her in death, if not in life.

"What if she had been speaking the truth?" Amit asks the question quietly.

This time the silence is broken by a babble of loud voices. In our town, everything is everybody's business and my fairytale marriage and nightmarish end has been the subject of endless speculation.

"What if, during the weekend when we all had gone to Shimla to celebrate the end of our law examination, something did happen? What if it is true?" Amit repeats softly. "What if she was raped and had no recollection of it?"

"Impossible," shrugs Dad, who is the best criminal lawyer in town, "it's absolutely impossible."

"It's possible," retorts Ritesh, my brother, a medical student, who loves trivia, "if it is date rape. The drug Rohypnol is commonly used for this purpose. It makes the person lose consciousness and she has no memory of what happened later."

"Ayesha panicked the next day, but later when it was suggested that she should undergo a medical examination to confirm the rape," says Amit, "she baulked at it, because she was traumatised by the thought of what would follow."

"But today the law has been amended; a rape victim no longer faces a harrowing interrogation," begins Justice Rajat Desai, and then stops.

"Exactly," exclaims Amit, "but not seven years ago. Ayesha as a law student knew what was in store for her in the courtroom. And she did not want to be mauled by lawyers and face a trial by the media. But the trauma of rape and suspicion began to kill her, she started looking at her classmates and wondering who it was. The discovery that she was pregnant and the abortion that followed must have been traumatic, especially as she had to handle it alone. It was enough to throw someone off the edge, and Ayesha was always sensitive. It was only a year later, when Nandini and I were getting married, that Ayesha acknowledged that she loved me and sent me a letter. I got it after she died. She must have waited for me the entire day and when I failed to arrive she must have assumed that I had rejected her."

Amit then takes out a piece of paper from his wallet, unfolds it carefully and says, "She wrote this letter to me before she died. Everyone knows that I loved Ayesha, I was crazy about her and I had proposed to her. But Ayesha could never make up her mind. She needed time. She was a small-town girl and a love marriage was almost unthinkable in her family. But I still hoped that she would say yes to me someday. But she had changed after that visit to Shimla. Something went wrong, radically wrong. None of us knew for sure; we could only guess. It is only when I decided to marry Nandini that Ayesha realised that she loved me after all. She asked me to see her at 5 pm, the day before our wedding, else she would end her life. I got the letter a day after our marriage, when I went to attend court."

I recollect the day so vividly. I had spent our wedding night consoling Amit, who sat dry-eyed as though cast in stone. He had left for office the next day in order to retain his sanity and had disappeared thereafter. Now I knew it was because of that letter.

"She mentioned in her letter that she knew that she had been raped, though she had no memory of it. She had tried to put it behind her, to forget it like a bad dream, because after all, she had no recollection of the rape at all, but the trauma of knowing that it had happened had brought her to the brink of a mental breakdown. She had been betrayed by someone known. She might have overcome the trauma over a period of time. But realising a month later that she was pregnant shattered her completely. The abortion that followed was equally traumatic."

"But...but this letter is only a photocopy," asserts Dad, holding the paper gingerly, as though its very touch could contaminate him.

"I assume she sent the original letter to my house, knowing that I had taken a week's leave for my wedding, but it was never found," shrugs Amit.

I wonder how he knew. Then I realise that, had the letter been found, it would have made news.

"I saw Ayesha in our house that day before Amit's wedding," says Suhana slowly.

But that fact would have surprised no one. We have always followed an open-door policy and been in and out of each other's houses every day. Even I had gone to Amit's house that very day.

"But who could have raped Ayesha?" Ritesh is stuck to the problem we all have tried to ignore. It is the result of his devouring crime fiction for breakfast, lunch and dinner. Or perhaps he had a crush on Ayesha as well. After all, Ayesha was so incredibly beautiful.

"Figure it out for yourself," suggests Amit, as if it is a conundrum he has given Ritesh to solve.

"The man who escorted her to her hotel room," Ritesh thinks aloud, slowly working out the sequence of events, "suggests he was the one who spiked her drink."

I glower at him. "It was Rajesh who escorted Ayesha," I say coldly, "and he had returned within five minutes of taking her to her room."

I knew, because Amit and I were waiting for him. I remember it all so well: Ayesha's asking for tomato juice while we all drank Bloody Marys, then her feeling giddy, nauseous and a bit drunk. Amit's offering to take Ayesha to her room but me dragging him to the dance floor, forcing Rajesh to accompany her, and Rajesh's return soon after escorting Ayesha to her room.

"You may be right," admits Ritesh, "but he could have taken the key with him when he left, especially if it was a card key, in which case the door is shut simply by pulling it hard. He could always return to her room later. If he was the one who had spiked her drink, he would have known that she would be unconscious for hours."

Rajesh begins to flush and I start wondering if that was how it had happened. Have I been sleeping with a rapist for the past two years?

The spotlight has shifted from Rajesh and me to Ayesha and Amit. It seems a repeat of the nightmare that had begun seven years ago. Amit has painted Ayesha in a new light, not as a girl crying wolf and falsely accusing her classmates of rape, but the victim of a date rape, who preferred to suffer in silence rather than seek justice because she knew that, if she tried, the defence lawyers would maul her in the courtroom.

But Ayesha died seven years ago. I am done with mourning her. It is time to begin where we had left off. My prayers have been answered. Amit has come back from the dead. This time I do not have to share him with anyone.

Rajesh looks at me with spaniel eyes but I glower at him in return. I do not know if he is a pet dog or a rabid dog who had raped Ayesha. The engagement party has ended very differently from what I had anticipated. But I am lucky. I have found my husband again. I am so grateful to God.

We return to my room late at night. My sister Ananya has littered rose petals from the bouquets of flowers I had received on the bed sheets. It makes for a beautiful bridal bed.

My heart beats faster at the thought of Amit and me together at last. Shall I tell him about Rajesh and me? Or shall I remain silent? Surely Amit did not expect me to remain a celibate all my life? I flush; perhaps he had done precisely that.

"You must take a bath," I tell Amit. He seems to be in need of one, despite his freshly shampooed hair.

I fill up the bathtub and throw in my favourite bathing salts. I also pull out my bathrobe and hand it over to him. Amit goes into the bathroom and I hear a loud splash as he enters the bathtub. My nerves begin to tingle in anticipation.

But something else gnaws at me. It is the half-censorious look Amit gave me in the hall. Did I say something about Ayesha that I was not supposed to know? I quickly tiptoe towards the jewellery box and withdraw a piece of paper from a white envelope. It is the letter Ayesha had written and left at Amit's house. I had purloined it from Amit's desk seven years ago, thinking that she was only "crying wolf" and fearing that if Amit saw the letter our marriage would be off.

Yes, she had written to Amit that she had kept the knowledge of her pregnancy and her subsequent abortion a secret, as she did not want anyone to malign her character. But after her death it had somehow become public. I should not have told Dad about the pregnancy, and everyone else as well. I should not have smeared her reputation. I feel trapped.

Suddenly someone tiptoes behind me. Amit asks, but there is no tenderness in his voice, "The original, I presume?"

The letter flutters and falls from my hand. He picks it up, reads it briefly and says, "It is always nice to have one's suspicions confirmed."

I look at him in surprise. Suspicions? Since when has he suspected? Since the time he found the photocopy of the letter seven years ago? Has he actually been in the Himalayas or was it wishful thinking on my part? Has he been practising law in some district all this time while ferreting around for the truth? Did he have a confidante—his sister Suhana, perhaps? Was that why he was able to return in the nick of time to stall my engagement? What does he intend to do now?

His next words confirm what I suspect. "I hope you know the punishment for abetment to suicide. Under Section 306 of the IPC..."

"Not abetment to suicide," I say hurriedly, "but suppression of evidence." I bite my lips as I say it. "You can't prove anything," I argue, but I think of Amit's implacable eyes. And the letter, smeared with my fingerprints, which I have been reading again and again. What madness had made me retain it? Why had I not torn it years ago?

"You can't prove anything," I repeat.

"Maybe not," he says, "but I shall make a damn good try."

I think of my fledgeling career and what this will do to it. I think of Amit, who has returned only to lock me into a loveless marriage. I wonder which of them is the greater punishment.

# A Ticket to Heaven

The fog hung across the Delhi skies like a grey curtain, reducing visibility to near zero.

"Hell," he swore to himself, "under these bad conditions, will a flight take off?" He had forgotten about the Delhi fog in December. Winter mornings, grey fog, delayed flights and missed connections. How could he have forgotten all this?

He had a sense of déjà vu as the past 10 years seemed to roll off him. Once again he became a pubescent youth who had set off on his journey to the unknown, amidst the fog, delayed flights and missed connections.

"Relax, Namit," said his younger brother Sheel, the voice of sanity. "Just chill. Things have changed in the last decade. Improved technology, you know. Delhi has night-landing facilities. The airport functions 24x7. Your flight will take off."

Namit shrugged, a cynic at the best of times when it came to inclement weather. He sat gingerly at the edge of the car seat, unable to sit back and relax, simply because Jaya was by his side. It began to rain just as they left the house. Large drops of rain hit the car roof and trickled down the car window, running in rivulets down the window pane. After the rains, the skies would clear. He relaxed at the thought.

As the car started from the driveway, Namit looked covertly at Jaya. He hoped that she had not begun to cry. He doubted if he could cope with a weeping bride. He was not good with people, not really. He felt awkward. Give me my computer, and a list of financial statistics, he said to himself, and I would feel completely at home.

Thankfully, Jaya was not crying. Her head was bent; only her hands were visible and the only sign of her distress at leaving India was the turning and twisting of her hands. He looked at her hands, long and slender, with fingers tapering into long, polished, pink nails. Talons, he thought wryly. It would not do to get on the wrong side of her. He looked surreptitiously at her hennaed palms, with their maze of whorls and swirls, announcing her bridal status, as did the vermillion on her forehead, the anklets on her feet and the gold-and-red glass bangles that filled up half her arms.

Namit looked out of the car window and sighed. It continued to drizzle. "Better get used to this weather, Jaya," he said ruefully, "It often rains like this in the USA."

She didn't speak, but merely nodded. Jaya was a shy, demure bride, Namit realised. He knew she would suit him fine. He often thought of himself as taciturn. A quiet wife would not demand conversation. "Are you nervous?" he tried talking to her again.

Again she nodded her head.

"It will be difficult to keep up a conversation if only I talk," he said, "You must say something."

"I am a good listener," she mumbled, hugging her knees, and he almost had to bend to hear her speak.

Sheel, sitting in the front of the car, put on his favourite song. "If you two have run out of conversation so soon, I think this might help."

Namit laughed. But with the raunchy *"kajara re, kajara re"* filtering into the car, Jaya relaxed and leaned back in the seat.

The driver drove slowly into the airport. When Namit stepped out he found himself being hugged by Amma and Papa, Sheel, Anu and his in-laws, while Jaya, with her back bent, was busy touching everyone's feet.

"Take care, look after Jaya and be good."

"Come and visit us next year and give us some good news."

He could hear a cacophony of voices. He grinned, wondering if Jaya could make any sense out of it, as he couldn't. But Jaya had probably not heard any of them. She was busy clinging to her mother and crying.

Namit felt heads turn when Jaya and he walked into the Air India Club Class counter. Jaya looked like a beautiful painting come alive. Her skin was like porcelain, her eyes large and lustrous, and her bearing regal. He was a slave to her beauty. This, he realised, is what it meant to fall in love, although his was an arranged marriage. Her wish was his command. She was a trophy wife, he admitted sheepishly to himself.

He could see the admiration in the eyes of the duty officer, who smiled at Jaya although he turned to him and said, "Have a nice trip, Sir."

The flight was on time and the two-hour wait went off quickly. Soon they were aboard the plane. A little later an air hostess came with glasses of fruit juice. He chose watermelon juice while she chose coconut water. He saw her sipping the juice, her long and swan-like neck thrown back a little.

"Have you been to New York before?" He knew the question was stupid even before he asked it. They both knew that her passport had been made only after their marriage was fixed.

She turned towards him and smiled. "How does the seat recline?" she asked instead.

He immediately turned towards her seat to do her bidding. Soon he was fiddling with the buttons, in his element while dealing with mechanical things, telling her how to recline the seat, teaching her how to use the television screen, passing on the in-flight magazine to her to browse.

She began to chuckle and he smiled, realising that he was behaving like an overprotective nanny indulging a five-year-old child.

Jaya Saxena—he rolled the name on his tongue. It sounded good. More importantly, it sounded right. It had a velvet feel to it. It had been right to wait, for he had found himself the perfect bride.

He had not been in the mood for marriage for years. He had his work, his internet, his music, the baseball games, and a few chosen friends. He had been unwilling to give up his cherished freedom.

"What kind of girl do you want to marry?" his sister Anu had asked him in desperation.

He had not dared to disclose the truth. He had not dared to tell Anu about the face that had haunted him in his dreams. The face that was straight out of Raja Ravi Varma's paintings. A hauntingly beautiful face, like Rani Padmini, like the queens of the olden times. He knew Anu would've laughed after hearing him. He was a staid investment banker who dealt in figures, one who delved in exchange rates. He could not be expected to turn lyrical about beauty.

His visit to Allahabad to see a potential bride had been undertaken only to indulge his mother. He did not want to marry a girl from a small town. But that was before Jaya had stepped into the drawing room.

"She is the one," he had said to himself, his wish of a computer professional, preferably foreign-qualified, going down the drain.

"Why isn't she married yet?" he asked wonderingly once he had said yes.

She was 25, and a girl as breathtakingly beautiful as her should have been snapped up long ago. He would have thought that guys would have queued up at her doorstep to ask for her hand.

"There were some whispers about her having a boyfriend. There was some problem of caste or religion," his aunt, the matchmaker, murmured.

His Dad coughed and said, "Do you like the match?"

Namit smiled. He was not concerned about Jaya's past. He knew that the future belonged to them.

Namit turned towards Jaya, his week-old bride, but she seemed engrossed in the in-flight magazine. "You will love Connecticut, where I live," he said.

"You don't live in New York, then?" she asked, her voice low-pitched.

"Not New York," he said, swallowing a bit. "New York is too expensive. I stay in Connecticut. I love the countryside. It helps me unwind when I leave the skyscrapers, the looming skyline, the serpentine traffic and the milling crowds and return home."

He loved the lush green trees that lined the roads, the lake near his house, the deer that scampered on his lawns at dawn, the strawberry and apple orchards nearby, where he hand-picked his choice of fruits. But he found it difficult to put all this into words.

"Tell me about yourself," he asked Jaya a trifle diffidently. They had been married five days, but he had lost her to the rituals and ceremonies and hoards of relations who had teased and bullied him, telling him that he had a lifetime to spend with her, but they had just a few days.

Jaya just shook her head shyly.

"Let me tell you about myself," he said and then stopped. How does one distill the essence of 28 years of existence into a few hours, he wondered. He knew that he could not do it. He did not have a way with words. Would she understand the pride and longing of his middle-class parents, who had mortgaged their house and raised student-education loans to indulge in his wish to study abroad? Would she understand his responsibilities towards his parents, and his need to repay the debt he owed them by taking on the responsibility of Sheel's education and Anu's marriage? Or would she baulk at the responsibilities? Would she be able to adjust to living alone throughout the day, and spend time in a lonely house all by herself?

Slowly he began to talk about the adjustments she would need to make. Then he felt her head touching his shoulder and saw that she was fast asleep. He smiled. He sat still, unwilling to move lest she got up, savouring the proximity.

She woke up in time for dinner, smiled at him shyly, and then walked up to the restroom to freshen up. He smiled with pleasure when he saw heads turn as she walked back. He thought of his marriage, when she had looked a vision in a pink lehenga-choli, with a golden filigree necklace on her neck.

"Standing beside her, I feel like an ugly duckling," he had joked to Anu. "I wonder what she saw in me."

"Don't worry, bro...you have a job in Citibank in New York," said Anu. "Women would fall all over you to marry you," she continued.

He grinned at his little sister, fiercely protective of her big brother, ready to discount his five-foot six-inch height and dusky complexion.

"Perhaps she saw your salary statement," said Sheel, taking a dig at him.

He flushed. Perhaps Sheel spoke the truth.

When Jaya woke up he slipped his hand into hers. It felt warm and comforting. They had not had time for a honeymoon. In fact, he recalled, flushing a little, the marriage had not been consummated yet. But it was better that way. In Connecticut, with no relations, no friends, they would have all the time in the world to themselves.

There was a change of aircraft at Frankfurt airport. He ushered her into the Swissair lounge, which was shared with the Air India passengers. She sat in the lounge, nibbling cheese biscuits and sipping tomato juice.

"You fell asleep when I was talking of the adjustments you would need to make," Namit said.

She looked at him and smiled. "You worry too much," she said. "My philosophy in life is que sera sera."

He smiled in turn. This was the longest speech she had made yet.

The flight landed in New York on time. The immigration did not take much time and their baggage arrived quickly at the baggage carousel.

"It's my lucky day," Namit told Jaya as he loaded the luggage onto the trolley. His cell phone began ringing as they stepped out of the arrival gate.

"We are waiting for you at the car park," he heard Swaminathan say.

"My friend Swaminathan is waiting for us at the car park," Namit told Jaya.

He saw Swaminathan striding towards him, a large bouquet of roses in his hand. "Give it to Jaya," he said, turning behind, but Jaya was not there. Where was she, he wondered.

He saw her running ahead to meet someone. He saw her fling her arms around him. Namit smiled indulgently. He was perhaps a cousin who had come to receive her. She had been too shy to tell him about her cousin. Jaya slipped her arm into his, and walked back towards Namit.

"Namit," she said, "meet Azeez, the man I love and wanted to marry but couldn't."

He looked at Azeez, who was almost his own height, with a wheatish complexion and glasses. Not the handsomest of men, he thought dispassionately, in fact, not even better-looking than him. But there was a difference between them. Jaya loved him.

"I am going with Azeez," Jaya said.

He felt as if he had been hit in the abdomen. The stab of pain was almost physical. His face was drained of colour. He thought he had heard wrongly. Jaya was his wife; she could not walk out on him like this. "But we are married; you are my wife," Namit said, the words sounding strange to his own ears.

"You can file for divorce," Jaya retorted. He saw Swaminathan looking at him pityingly and then looking away. Then he looked at Jaya once again. "But why?" he asked her. Why did Jaya go through the farce of a marriage? He deserved an explanation even if he did not need it.

Suddenly he was struck by an explanation. The reason a girl as beautiful as Jaya had remained unmarried, the reason she had said yes to his proposal. The sudden stomach cramps she had suffered after her marriage, which had left their marriage unconsummated. He had given into her wishes, thinking that they had a lifetime together. And now this.

Jaya understood his unspoken question. "Papa did not allow me to marry Azeez," she said. "He forced us to break up. For three years I turned down all marriage proposals, but when you arrived it was different. I changed my mind because you lived in the USA and it was the only way I could be with Azeez. I am sorry."

She stepped forward and thrust something into his hand. And then she was gone.

He looked at the piece of paper. It was her ticket to the US. He saw her receding back and realised that was all what he meant to her. A ticket to the US.

# Love thy Neighbour

It was the rasping that woke her up. The harsh sound that comes from laboured breathing, as though of a travel-weary trekker climbing a mountain, or an athlete on the last leg of a marathon, or a man making love. She did not realise the walls between the two houses were so porous.

There was something familiar about the sounds. She felt as though she had heard them before. Suddenly she heard a muffled scream, as though smothered. A woman moaning in pleasure or a woman choking to death? The cry reverberated throughout her being.

She got up from her bed. "Ramu," she tried to call, "Ramu." But the words stuck in her throat. Was Ramu deaf? Or was her imagination working overtime? She looked at the wall separating the two houses. It seemed thick, really thick, as though it was impossible for any sound to escape through it. Yet she had heard the smothered cry. For a moment she contemplated going down the stairs and up to the gate. But she saw, through the window, the thin sliver of a moon, and knew that it was late. She peered at the luminous dial of her watch and realised that it was five past two. She closed her eyes and tumbled back into bed.

The next morning, she got up languidly, a curious stiffness pervading her limbs. She had forgotten to shut the air conditioner at night and her tired limbs could no longer take the change between hot and cold with equanimity.

"Old, I am becoming old," she mumbled, as she peered into the dressing-table mirror. Strands of pepper-grey hair tumbled all around her face. A few months ago, her hair had not been touched by grey, there had been no frown lines or crow's feet on her face, and she had not been afraid to face the mirror with her glasses on. A few months ago, Anant was alive.

Sunlight was streaming through the window now, but she still lacked the energy to get up. "If only," she thought, "I could curl up in my bed and die."

It was only when Ramu brought her a cup of black tea with a twist of lemon that she was able to get up from bed. It was yet another day to be faced, she thought to herself, which blended into a series of days, which made up a calendar year. Each had nothing to distinguish itself from the other; all were colourless and bland and frightening in their monotony.

After a while she decided to go for a walk. "My morning constitutional," she said to herself, but she wondered whom she was deceiving. As she reached the gate she saw her neighbour. His bearing was still regal despite the silver at his temples. His face in profile, she thought to herself, looked like a hawk's. He looked predatory. He was digging in his garden. Digging. A shiver passed through her.

"What are you digging?" she asked, her voice suddenly quite shrill.

He turned towards her in surprise. This was perhaps the first time she had spoken to him in months.

"A flower bed, of course," he said. "What did you think it was, Mrs Banerjee—a grave?" He laughed loudly, in a sound that was not unpleasant, but she turned white at his remark. So did he, when he realised what he had said. "I am sorry, Mrs Banerjee, really sorry," he mumbled, but she had fled into her house. He looked at her with anxiety. The poor woman was not all there, not since she had lost her husband.

She rushed into her room, buried her face into the pillow and started sobbing. She knew that her neighbour thought she was mad. She could see the pity in his eyes. "Poor Mrs Banerjee, mad, quite mad, ever since her husband died"—she knew that was what he thought, as did the others. But he did not know the truth. She did.

It had been a night like this, about six months ago. Except that it was May. The heat had been unbearable. She had woken up suddenly at the sound of a rasping noise. As though of a mountaineer climbing a mountain…an athlete running a marathon…or a man making love. There has been something familiar about the sounds and the voice, as though she had known it before, and then there had been a woman's muffled scream, as though someone had put his hand over her mouth to arrest it. She had groped at Anant for reassurance. The bed was empty.

She had then plucked the torch that lay beneath Anant's pillow and had made her way quietly to the door. It was not bolted. She had then gone slowly down the stairs and waited at the last step by the gate. Almost 15 minutes later, she had seen Anant emerge from the neighbour's house. He had seen her first as a shadow in the dark and then realised who she was. He had tried to catch hold of her, but she had fled. She had raced into the bedroom and shut the door from inside and made a great show of bolting it.

She had waited for him to bang at the door, and to demand entry into the bedroom. But he had done nothing. "Sated," she had thought, spitting out venom at him, "sated and probably fast asleep."

She had curled into fetal position and rocked herself to sleep. But sleep was long in the coming. How long had it been going on? How long had she been blind? Did the neighbour's husband know? These thoughts had continued to torment her. She had only been able to sleep properly in the early hours of the morning.

Only when Ramu had brought her black tea with a slice of lemon had she woken up.

"Where is Sahib?" she had asked Ramu, her eyes red from the tears and the sleepless night.

He had looked at her in surprise. He assumed that Anant was in the bathroom.

She had then walked into his study and banged on the door. Banged and banged yet again. When there had been no response she had panicked, and when Ramu had broken open the door she had a sense of foreboding of what awaited her.

Anant was swinging from the ceiling fan like a puppet, his face bloated, his eyes popping out, a grotesque caricature of the man he had once been. In his pocket had been a note saying, "I am sorry, Mona."

She could not get that image out of his mind, Anant swinging from the rope, his own judge, jury, and executioner.

The neighbour's wife, whose muffled cries had rocked her world, had not even bothered to come to console her. She had gone out of town on the pretext of work, leaving her to mourn the death of her husband, who, in the eyes of the world, had been goodness personified.

Her neighbours and friends had looked at her strangely. To them, she was a woman who had driven her husband to his death. She could not tell them the truth and besmirch his memory when his sin was that he had been weak. Didn't they say that one should not speak ill of the dead?

She had had her first nervous breakdown soon after. That was when she had begun to remain confined to her house, when her other neighbours had begun to say, "Poor Mrs Banerjee, she is not quite there, not since her husband died."

"Where is your wife?" she asked her neighbour the next time she saw him digging away in his garden.

"She is abroad," he said, his voice guarded, as though unwilling to say anything that could provoke a fresh outburst from her.

She sighed. Ever since Anant's death she had not seen Mita. She seemed to have disappeared somewhere, mourning her loss in private. Or had Anant meant nothing to her? Was he just one amongst a series of lovers, someone to share the night with whilst her husband was away?

She turned her thoughts towards the present. She looked at her neighbour's hands on the shovel and was fascinated by his wrists. They seemed strong and capable of anything, even murder. "I am going to join my wife within a fortnight," he added.

"And the house?" she asked, trying to ferret out nuggets of information like an overzealous squirrel.

"Oh, we will vacate it," he said.

"You are planning to leave forever?" Even she was amazed at her inquisitiveness.

"Quite so," he said, and, turning his back towards her, went back to his digging.

It rained a week later. Tumultuous rain wreaked havoc in the overgrown jungle that had once been her garden. It was a sudden downpour that turned her neighbour's garden into slush, a pool of water replacing what had been a bed of flowers. From her terrace she peered at the newly laid out flower bed with interest. She even thought she saw something.

Her heart began to palpitate. She went and fetched a pair of binoculars from Anant's study, and looked through them at the garden. It was just a white rag. She turned away, disappointed. What had she expected? That a skeletal hand would pop out of the flower bed like in an old Hindi movie? The voices she had heard had been a part of her overwrought imagination. Ever since Anant had died, something in her mind had become unhinged. She had begun to doubt everything and everyone. She slumped her shoulders and walked away.

From his window her neighbour saw the flower bed turn slushy. He knew that it had been a close shave. He was glad he had not followed his original intention of burying his wife Mita's body beneath the flower bed. He knew Mrs Banerjee would snoop. He had seen her snoop on that fateful night when he had arrived unexpectedly, late at night on foot, his taxi with its punctured tyre stranded across the road, and seen Anant emerge silently from his house.

Mita had not known, but he had, as had Anant's wife, why he had died. It seemed unfair that Anant had to pay for his infidelity with his life while Mita went scot-free. He decided that she too had to pay the price, sooner or later. He chose later.

It had been simple, really. He thought it would be poetic justice to end her life on the bed, where it had all begun. So one night, after she returned from a trip abroad, when she had clung to him, her lips parted, her eyes bright, her body arched, he had simply coiled his fingers around her throat and squeezed the life out of her, smothering her cry with his large hand. He had not known that the walls of his house were so porous. Or perhaps his neighbour was fey.

He was glad that at the last minute he had changed his mind about where to bury her. Instead of the flower bed he had dragged his wife's corpse from the deep freeze and buried it inside the garage. Luckily the snoopy Mrs Banerjee could not see the garage from inside and discover the newly plastered bricks on the floor in the corner. Someday, someone could find out the truth, if maybe an earthquake occurred, or if a tornado tore the house apart. But that would not matter to him if it happened once he was dead.

# Death

The smell of formalin assailed Sapna's nostrils. The ordeal of dissection was before her.

"Better watch out, Sapna; this will be your first cadaver," laughed Abhinav.

On hearing his words, Sapna felt bile rise into her mouth. She hated death. She had seen it recently at close quarters when her dad, who had lived in the twilight zone between life and death for three months, had finally succumbed to it. Death was ugly, Sapna knew. But she had to face it every day. This was her profession.

"A profession not of my choosing," a voice nagged within her. It was a profession she had chosen in order to fulfil a promise.

Rajeev would be a doctor when he grew up. That had been her father's dream. He had spun simple, uncomplicated dreams, and made a wish list. The son, a doctor. The daughter, a lecturer. His dreams took no account of his son, his expectations, abilities or desires.

"You'll get used to dissections," said Sharat lightly. "My brother Asit said that after some days he could leave his lunch box itself on the cadaver and not be squeamish about eating from it."

Sapna shivered at the very thought of it. Words of protest rose from within her but seeing the expression on Sharat's face, she realised that he was displaying a false sense of bravado. Beneath those bantering words he too looked ill at ease.

If only Rajeev had fulfilled the family expectations, Sapna would have been free to choose her own life and chase her own dreams, to explore the world, to travel into the unknown, to cross the turbulent seas, to soar in the skies, to lead a nomadic existence, rootless but infinitely fulfilling.

Suddenly the cover on the cadaver was pulled away.

"What a handsome young man," exclaimed Rashika, a catch in her voice.

They all turned around and looked. Sapna then saw the face and the world seemed to spin before her. If Amit had not held her just then she would have fallen.

"Take it easy, Sapna," said Abhinav, his arm thrown tenderly around her.

Bile rose in her mouth once again. She rushed out to the bathroom and retched. Rashika rushed in after her, looking concerned. "If I didn't know you so well, I would have suspected that you were pregnant," she said half-jokingly.

"I'll be alright," Sapna murmured, her face wan.

"What happened?" everyone asked curiously once she returned into the dissection hall.

"Nothing," Sapna muttered, and seeing their disbelieving looks she said, "He reminded me of my brother, Rajeev."

She knew she could no longer work on this table. She would never be able to retain her composure if she did so. She would have to tell the professor about it. There was a hushed silence around her. Her friends had heard about her brother. They also knew about her father's death.

"Take it easy," said the demonstrator. "Today you can just stand and watch."

Sapna thought of Rajeev, who with his golden looks was a painter's dream come true. His sonorous and honeyed voice reminded her at times of an eagle in flight and at other times of a cascading waterfall. Rajeev, who loved art, who loved all beautiful things, who should have been left to dabble in them, instead of being drawn into the grim world of competition.

The dissection was progressing smoothly; she could hear the voice of the demonstrator droning. She willed herself to pay attention to him, but her mind was far away.

She remembered the burden of hope on Rajeev's slender shoulders and then the result of his Class X examinations, which had disappointed their middle-class parents, who had seen their dreams threaten to crumble.

"Never mind," his father had said, "Rajeev will do better in the Class XII examinations."

Their father had arranged for tuitions for Rajeev in all subjects, as well as rigorous coaching for the Medical entrance examination.

"Sapna," Rajeev had asked despairingly, "why doesn't Papa understand that I don't want to be a doctor; I can't be a doctor. I hate Physics and Maths. Why can't they accept that I am an average student?

"You have the brains in the family," Rajeev had added. "All I want to do is sing."

And he sang at all functions—community functions, school functions, everywhere. But the trophies and prizes he won seemed to mock him when his father sneered at his musical talent.

She remembered his poor performance in the Class XII examinations, and his subsequent failure to clear the Medical entrance examination. She shuddered as she recalled their father doing the unthinkable, taking his belt and whipping Rajeev in his disappointment.

The next day Rajeev walked out of his home, never to return. He left behind no note. She could never forget the frantic calls to the police, the newspaper advertisements, the search for Rajeev in the hospitals, the morgue, in fact everywhere. She had alternated between hope and despair, wondering if Rajeev would suddenly return one day, just as he had gone, waiting for the postman, wondering if the mail would bring a letter from her brother; sitting by the phone, waiting for a call from him, letting days slip into months and months into years.

She saw her father shrivel up, his eyes dimmed with tears. After his sudden heart attack, she promised her parents that she would take the place of the son who had let them down, that she would fulfil their dreams and look after them once her father retired.

She had worked day and night for a dream which was not hers, compensated by the glint of happiness when her father cried pathetically on seeing her roll number among those who had successfully qualified for the Medical entrance test. She regretted his bus accident, after which he battled for survival for three months before he succumbed to his injuries. Since then she had lived a life of abject loneliness, with a despondent mother, within a lonely house.

The dissection was over at last.

"It wasn't so bad, was it?" asked the demonstrator kindly. "Next time, Sapna, you will have to do it yourself."

She nodded dumbly as she walked behind Abhinav, Rashika and Sharat from the dissection hall.

It was late by the time Sapna reached home. Her mother, a perpetually fatigued look on her face, stood at the door. For how many years had she stood like that, hoping that Rajeev would walk through the door one day?

"I've kept a fast," her mother said.

"For what?" asked Sapna.

"It's *Sakat Chauth*; it's a fast for the long life of a son," said her mother. "Have you forgotten?"

"You have no son," responded Sapna. "Your son left you four years ago."

"I have Rajeev," said her mother. "Wherever he is, he must be fine."

"Ma," Sapna sounded fatigued, "if he was alive, he would have got in touch with us; why do you not accept that he is dead?"

"What has happened to you?" asked her mother angrily. "Why are you talking this way? He is alive. My heart says so."

Sapna thought of the body lying on the dissection table. It was Rajeev, her brother. She thought of the guilt that had assailed her throughout the afternoon that she was doing an injustice to her brother by not revealing his identity, by letting him remain an unclaimed body, by not giving him the cremation he deserved. Some unknown force seemed to have sealed her lips, preventing her from blurting out the truth.

Seeing his face in repose, she had wondered about the last four years of his life. Where had he gone? To Mumbai, to chase his dream of becoming a playback singer? Or had he become a member of some gang? How had he survived all these years? Why did he never return home? How had he died? Why had he died?

There were many questions that would remain unanswered. She knew that she would always carry the guilt of knowing that, by not acknowledging her dead brother, by denying his existence, she had denied him the right to die with dignity. But she had chosen to keep silent because of her mother, who lived on the hope that Rajeev was alive and would return home one day. It was a false hope, but a hope nevertheless. Sapna knew that she had been right not to cheat her mother of it.

"Forgive me, Rajeev," Sapna said quietly, "but you're the hope Ma lives on for. For her sake, I will have to keep you alive."

Her mother came and put a hand on her head. "Come, *beti*, come for the puja, and pray for the long life of your brother."

Sapna saw the flickering diya, like the flickering hope in her mother's eyes. She saw her mother take the *roli* and put a tika on her forehead.

As her mother began to chant a prayer, Sapna put her head down, so that her mother would not see her tears spill and mingle with the vermillion in the silver thali.

# The Atonement

It was the 8th of March, International Women's Day. The date seemed to dance before her eyes. Today was the day of celebration of women's rights, which had its origin in the movement for women's suffrage. Today was the day of the celebration of women's equality. And what a struggle it had been. Every concession had to be fought for; nothing came for free. After independence had started another struggle—the struggle for women's independence.

As she stepped onto the podium the irony of the situation was not lost on her. Hysteria began to bubble inside her throat, like the fizz of a cola. She was afraid that it would erupt suddenly, like molten lava, shaming her before the large audience. The sea of faces began to swim before her. Words seemed to choke inside her throat. She dug her teeth into her lower lip and drew blood. She licked it slowly, the peculiar taste quite alien to her tongue.

When she began her address, it was in her well-modulated voice. "International Women's Day owes its origin to the movement for women's suffrage. We have come a long way since then, haven't we?"

Her opening remarks were followed by a pregnant silence. She knew that she had caught the attention of the audience. "We are never tired of saying that India gave to the world its second woman prime minister. We pay homage to Indian-born Kalpana Chawla, whose space odyssey has left an indelible mark on the younger generation and who shall shine like a luminous star in the Indian firmament. We revel in the success of Karnam Malleswari, who was the first woman to bring India an Olympic medal. We applaud Bachendri Pal and Santosh Yadav for scaling Mount Everest. We bask in the success of Arundhati Roy and Kiran Desai's literary marvels. And we pretend that this is the real India. But it is not.

"The truth," she said, "is infinitely less palatable. The truth is that, in India, women remain children of a lesser god. One third of India's women are illiterate. While education opens a window to the world, the unlettered woman remains mired in darkness. She has no identity of her own. Most of the time she is just a left-thumb impression on official documents."

Thunderous applause greeted her words.

She waited for the applause to die down. Then she continued. "The 2011 Census shows that the child sex ratio in India is 918—the lowest in the country since independence, pointing an invidious finger to the most heinous of all crimes: female foeticide."

She saw the audience cringe. "This phenomenon is not confined to the poor. It is in fact more prevalent among the affluent. Education has nothing to do with it," she said, her face a mask of fury. "Let us simply face facts. A girl child is seldom wanted.

"Just the other day, there was a report in the newspaper that a man drowned his eight-year-old daughter in the river." She continued, "Her crime? That she was a girl. She was not his only child. He had a three-year-old male child as well. But for eight long years, while she grew up, he continued to resent her, until his resentment climaxed in her drowning. This obsession with a male child must not continue."

There was a hushed silence in the hall as people hung onto every word that she uttered. Today, however, she had difficulty in speaking. A wave of nausea struck her. Her pallor went grey. Rivulets of sweat began to trickle down her face. "A few days ago, there was a newspaper report about a man who buried his newborn alive. The infant's crime? Again, she was a girl. Her mother could not bear it and complained to the police. The police dug around the site and found the child alive. God alone knows," she shuddered, "if the lack of oxygen had caused the girl any brain damage."

This time silent sobs began to rack her body even as sweat poured down.

"She is so impassioned in her speech. See, she has begun shivering," whispered someone in the front row.

She struggled hard, and clenched her hands to retain her composure and control the waves of nausea that hit her again and again.

She walked out of the hall soon after her speech was over, amidst stunned silence and then overwhelming applause. Clutching the bouquet of roses she had received, she buried her head in their fragrance. Ravindra was in his car, with the front door slightly ajar.

"Come, darling," he said, trying to hide his impatience beneath the veneer of a smile.

She sat in the car and he started it even before she had fastened her seat belt. He seemed to be in a tearing hurry. As the car rushed forward she looked at the traffic around her and muttered to herself, "Millions die, millions die in traffic accidents every day. Then why does it hurt so much?"

They stopped beside the Mehta Nursing Home 20 minutes later. She walked into the hospital and was soon allotted a room.

"It will be over soon; it will be over in a few hours," said Ravindra, his boyish face lighting up with a smile, as he squeezed her arm ever so slightly.

Listen," she said hesitantly, "perhaps we should reconsider our decision."

"No," he said emphatically, his voice stern, "my decision is final. We don't want another child."

Her eyes went bleak. "If that was so, why did we need a sonography?" The question died on her lips, as had several others before it. Would things have been different had their firstborn been a son? But arguing with her husband was useless. His word was final. She had learnt it the hard way.

The irony of her situation hit her once again. She, the arch feminist, the outspoken advocate for gender equity, had come to the hospital to abort her female child. When they wheeled her in the operating theatre all she sought was oblivion, from pain, from doubts and from guilt.

Waves of nausea began to hit her when she returned to consciousness.

"It's the aftermath of the anaesthesia," said the doctor.

Bleary-eyed, she watched her husband by her side.

"It's over," he said, "it's all over."

"Yes," she parroted, "it's all over."

But he did not know and she had no intention of telling him the truth immediately. She had not just aborted her female child. She had also undergone a laparoscopic tubectomy, to ensure that she bore no more children, either male or female. The first was her compulsion. The second, her atonement.

# Dead End

India Gate in New Delhi is a walker's paradise. Seeing it through the pink haze of the morning mist, I am reminded of the Arc de Triomphe, except of course there is no Champs-Elysees nearby and no roadside cafes spilling over with people till the wee hours of the morning. India Gate is surrounded by many arterial roads. I am bleary-eyed when I begin my morning walk. Late nights take their toll, as do soft contact lenses, which deprive my eyes of oxygen and do not let my eyes breathe. Vanity, however, prevents me from wearing my glasses, which have become thicker with the passage of time,

However, mornings are different. I am sleepy and but for the alarm I would curl up and sleep, hugging the lavender body pillow I received as a free gift with a magazine subscription. There is something very reassuring about the pillow. It is cuddly and soft, like a teddy bear, not hard and curved, like the small of a man's back. It allows me to hug and caress it. It makes no demands in turn. It is in this bleary-eyed state that I don my shoes, socks, and salwar-kameez, and put on my lenses to go for my walk. I am alone, of course. Sushant is away; he has been in the USA for three years. But his habits have remained with me. And I need the exercise. What will he say when he returns and finds that his wife has turned obese?

I can do the morning walk almost blindfolded. From Zakir Hussain Marg, I walk on the pavement adjoining the Children's

Park. It takes me five minutes to walk to the end of the park, turn back, take the turn towards the National Stadium and then return. Next, of course, is Tilak Marg, and then Kasturba Gandhi Marg. After that I turn towards Rajpath and then towards Shah Jahan Road and finally I return to Zakir Hussain Marg to return to my house. Six turns in 60 minutes. I have timed it perfectly.

People use this time for communion with God. I have heard walkers chant mantras under their breath while they walk. Others hum bhajans. I don't. I am too practical. I find comfort in people. Maybe I am lonely and am missing Sushant. It has been three years since he left. During this time he has come to India just thrice.

It is tough living without him, even though some people think that, at 35, the geographical separation doesn't matter any more. Although I haven't talked much to other morning walkers, I know some people by their name and face.

There is someone whose name I don't know. I have nicknamed her Kashish. There is something sylphlike about her. In my more fanciful moments I imagine that she is some aquatic creature, perhaps a mermaid, who has emerged out of the fountain at India Gate. Or perhaps she is a wood nymph who lurks in the green foliage of the park.

She has high cheekbones and pale cream skin. She has beautiful black eyes. She is tall and slim. She mystifies me because unlike other women who try to fit into jeans and tee shirts or salwar-kameezes, she always comes clad in a saree and blouse, wearing Nike shoes along with them. She seems oblivious to the amused glances that follow her. She always wears a crushed cotton saree and I suspect that she doesn't wear a nightdress at night and wears the same saree instead.

She gets up in the morning and, without changing her clothes, comes for her morning walk. This explains her crumpled sarees. I think, although I am only guessing, that her husband has deserted her and that is why she is so careless about her appearance.

One of the regulars on the walk is a pot-bellied man with a polythene bag full of bajra. He throws fistfuls of bajra as he walks, making all the crows congregate and fly so low that one even sat on my head. It is said that a crow sitting on one's head doesn't augur well for the future. Perhaps that is true. I thought that the man was a social worker, or a compulsive bird lover, until it struck me that it is more likely that the pundits told him to perform this religious rite, to ward off some evil spirits. *Daan punya*, you know. As though you can appease the gods this way.

Another regular walker is a tall man with thinning hair. He comes marching vigorously. Perhaps he belongs to the laughter club, for he works himself into laughter, but the laughter is not spontaneous at all; it is forced, and mirthless, as though he is laughing at life itself. Perhaps he is laughing only on the doctor's orders. Often he slips into a morose silence and walks with his head down. He has a butterfly mark on his shoulder. He occasionally looks up. Whenever he walks past me I get a whiff of his cologne, which smells of tangerines. The intensity of his gaze is searing. I keep thinking that maybe his wife has died. It is a pity I can't ask him now. I was told only today that he died. It is difficult to imagine him dead. I can still see him, his hands swinging by his side, his gaze piercing.

Finally there is Baiju. I don't know why I call him that, except that he reminds me of the old-time actor Bharat Bhushan in the film *Baiju Bawra*. Baiju's face is almost completely covered with a beard; his head too is covered with thick matted hair, which has reached his shoulders. I suspect that there are hundreds of lice crawling within those locks, but of course I don't really know. He remains bare-bodied even in winter; all he has is a loincloth around him, in deference to people's sensibilities, I guess. He sits on a bench outside the Children's Park. At times he sleeps with the lungi crawling up his knees. His legs appear to be sinewy, with well-developed calf muscles. That is surprising, since he seems to sleep on the bench all day long. He mustn't have bathed for days or months. He must smell. Of course I don't know that. I haven't come that close to him. He has no begging bowl in his hand. I suspect, but it is only my suspicion, that he scrounges around the rubbish bins when the park is deserted, and eats from the leftover paper plates of chaat. I see him every morning when I walk through the park like a somnambulist. How old is he? Not more than 30 years if his black hair is anything to go by.

There are many rumours about him. Some people claim that he is an escaped lunatic. His story is rather commonplace but sad. Some years ago he went abroad for his studies, leaving behind his beloved. When he returned to India he found that she had committed suicide after being forced to marry someone else. It made him lose his sanity.

This story does not ring quite true, does it? Quite right. I made it up, and since I lacked inspiration I used the storyline of the old film *Khilona*. It wasn't bad as stories go, was it?

The truth, I learnt, is more heart-wrenching. He was actually a war-weary soldier who returned home from war to find his wife with her lover. It broke him completely. He lost his sanity and killed them both. This one has a familiar ring too, right? I borrowed this from the film *Achanak*. Actually, I do not know who he is and every time I see him I imagine different things. Maybe he is an amnesic prince in the wilderness. Maybe he is a fugitive from justice. Who knows?

Once I did have an encounter with him. It was a late winter evening and I was returning from the government dispensary where I work as a doctor. I was leaving for the USA the next day, to be with my husband Sushant. It was a sort of emergency. A health problem of sorts. I had to walk home because my car had been sent to the garage for repairs and there was an autorickshaw strike that day. I began to walk from Kasturba Gandhi Marg towards India Gate. Crossing the road was not difficult. There was hardly any traffic on that cold winter evening. India Gate looked deserted. I did not see any people around. I just saw shadows. I walked slowly and passed India Gate where the Amar Jawan Jyoti lit bright. The flame gave me courage in the dark. But the one-and-a-half-kilometre long walk had left me tired. I sat on the bench by the side of the park. Suddenly I heard a voice say, "Hullo, so you have come at last."

I shifted uneasily in the shadows. The voice seemed to come from behind me.

"You can't leave me and go away—not when we have so much going between us. I won't let you leave me. I will tell him, I will tell him the truth, that it is not he but I who is..."

Blackmailer, a blackmailer. I shivered in disgust. Blackmailers deserved to die. Noiselessly I left the bench.

After a while I saw Baiju. He was not lying on his usual bench. He was walking. I had never seen him walking before. He looked tall, dark and fearsome. I increased my pace, and then looked back. There was no one on the road except us. The vein by my temple began to throb. My heart began to pound. I looked at my feet. I realised I was wearing sandals, not shoes.

I couldn't run, but I needed to. As I turned the corner I saw him give chase. In a blinding flash I understood who he was—a serial killer. Obviously, this was not his first time. But I could not give up so easily. I stepped out of my sandals, clutched them in my hands and ran. By this time I had crossed the park and come out to the main road. I saw him come closer. But now I was safe. Even in this severe winter, there were a couple of cars passing by and a couple of pedestrians on the road.

Without a word he came near me, dropped something by my feet, and left. I saw him depart and then bent down and looked. It was my passport. I picked it up with trembling hands. When I turned around, he was gone.

The next morning I left for a three-month vacation to the USA. I missed all the excitement of finding the body at India Gate. Yes, it was the tall man with the piercing gaze and thinning hair. It was the first thing people talked about when I returned to India and came for my walk. He had died unexpectedly the night before I had left.

"Heart attack?" I asked a fellow walker.

"The police suspect foul play. They think someone just pressed his carotid artery long enough," she said.

"How could someone do that?" I asked.

"A man could have come and put his arms around him from behind," shrugged the walker. "A woman could have done it from the front as well. All one needs to know is the right pressure point. A doctor or a nurse would know it easily."

I shuddered. His body was found near the bench on which I had been sitting. I knew that it was his voice I had heard. I had been so close to him that night. So close, and then, a little while later, he had died.

I kept walking on the road, engrossed in my own thoughts, patting my slightly swelling stomach gently. The emergency was over. I was over two months pregnant now, officially. And babies were known to be born premature. An abortion had not been an option for me. I was too old and it was too late anyway.

Then I saw Baiju lying on the bench. A wave of guilt passed over me. I owed him a word of gratitude for giving me back my passport. I had no idea where I had dropped it. But without it I couldn't have caught my flight the next day. I tried to smile at him and even tried to mouth a "thank you". He looked at my face and then turned his back towards me. I thought I saw an expression of hurt on his face. Or maybe it was fear.

# If Only

Every story should have a beginning, a middle and an end. This one doesn't, because I strayed into it in the middle and left without knowing the end. And yet it was cataclysmic enough to leave a profound impact on me. I grew up in those 15 minutes at 3.45 pm, when I stood in the middle of the road, flailing my arms, trying to stop a passing car, any car...

Or perhaps it started before that, at 11.30 am that Sunday morning, when I rang Prateek's doorbell, smelling romance in the air when all I should have smelt was milk turned sour in the rubbish bin outside, and the odour of asafoetida proclaiming that the inmates of the flat next to his were pure vegetarians.

Prateek opened the door—not the jean-clad Prateek I expected, but Prateek in his rumpled kurta-pyjamas, his hair ruffled, remnants of breakfast sticking to the corner of his mouth, and bits of ketchup on his kurta. "Vandita." He looked genuinely surprised and my heart began to sink as my voice acquired an accusatory note.

"You have forgotten," I muttered, and my voice got shriller. "You have forgotten that we were planning to see *Kabhi Alvida Naa Kehna* today."

He looked troubled as he ran his fingers through his tousled hair—a gesture that usually brought waves of tenderness in me but today only served to irritate me—and said, "I had to complete a presentation for a client tomorrow. I clean forgot."

I slumped into his armchair and snorted in anger. This was not the first time. It happened week after week. His work as an assistant manager in a multinational corporation, his targets and his need to accomplish them, all took priority over me.

"Vandita, try to understand," he pleaded, "we will go next week, I promise".

I got up. I had tried to understand, these past many months, not once but several times, when he had ordered chicken rolls and Diet Pepsi from the restaurant nearby, and I had watched movies on the video while he worked on his projects, before we wound up in bed. But today, I was in reckless mood. "Well, good luck," I taunted, "I am going to watch *Kabhi Alvida Naa Kehna*."

"Alone?" he asked, amazed.

"Yes, alone," I retorted sharply as I smoothened my salwar-kameez.

"You can't watch a movie alone," he countered, as though I would be guilty of income tax evasion or something even more serious. "You must be joking."

"I have never been more serious in my life," I retorted coldly as I began to unbolt the door.

"Tell you what," he suggested pleadingly, "I will order…"

"Chicken rolls and Diet Pepsi from the restaurant downstairs," I mimicked. "No thanks."

He shrugged his shoulders helplessly and I banged the door shut, making the pots of money plants he had kept on the ledge fall down to the ground. The door shuddered. A curious head popped out of the neighbour's kitchen as I walked down, my heels clattering on the staircase. Every once in a while I craned my neck to see if Prateek had followed me, and then hid my disappointment with a smile, on realising that he hadn't.

I took an autorickshaw to the theatre and stood in the queue, feeling awkward at the thought of being alone in the cinema hall.

"Two tickets, miss?" asked the man at the counter.

"One," I clarified. This was the time for financial prudence, not pretence. He looked at me appraisingly and sneered. Prateek had been right. After all, how many women saw movies alone? I clutched the corner-seat ticket I had bought and glanced furtively at my watch, and occasionally at the door, pretending that I had been stood up by my escort. I rushed into the theatre just when the door opened.

A young man entered the hall 15 minutes later, just when the credit titles had begun to roll, stood by my side helplessly, then walked up to the usher, returned immediately and asked me hesitatingly, "Is the next seat yours too?"

I shook my head and he gave a sigh of relief and sat down beside me, and I wondered what had made him come to the movie hall alone. But perhaps the rules were not the same for men and women. I sat stiffly throughout the first half, afraid of being alone in the movie hall, but I need not have worried. He did not even speak to me.

During the interval he got up and asked me, "Want something to eat?" and I muttered, "Popcorn and Coke," which is what I always said to Prateek whenever we watched a film. He returned 15 minutes later with an extra-large bag of popcorn and a can of Coke and whispered conspiratorially, "That's 145 rupees."

I grimaced in disgust. On the rare occasions we came to see movies, Prateek always paid for everything. I gave my neighbour the money and scowled some more. I realised that I would not have money for taking an autorickshaw back on my return, unless I hit an ATM. I would have to take a bus.

At 3.30 pm I walked out of the movie hall and stood at the deserted bus stop, wondering where everyone else had gone. Did all other movie goers have cars? Then I saw the guy sitting next to me in the cinema hall walking smilingly towards me.

"Hi!" he shouted enthusiastically, as though we were old friends meeting after many years and not cine-goers who had parted from each other just minutes ago.

"Hi! Which bus goes to Model Town?" I asked, hoping he would know.

"Bus." He frowned as though trying to remember; then suddenly his face cleared and he said, "A minibus."

A minibus came around the corner just then and he rushed onto the middle of the road and, flapping his arms like a bird, tried to flag down the bus.

But the bus simply rammed into him and I saw his body fly eight feet away and hit a lamp post. I screamed as I rushed to the spot, kneeled near his blood-splattered face, saying, "You'll be alright, you know," although I suspected that he was already dead.

A few cars whizzed past me but no one stopped. I went through his pockets, found his cell phone, rang up the police and the ambulance and waited till they arrived. When the policeman arrived, he looked quizzically at me, and asked, "How did it happen, miss? Was he your boyfriend?" I looked him straight in the eye and told him everything. Nikhil Bharadwaj was his name. I accompanied the policeman in the ambulance to the hospital where they noted, "Brought in dead," and even accompanied him to his house.

In that constricted DDA flat at Munirka that seemed suffocating because of the crowd that had gathered, I murmured, "In a kind of way I am to blame; if I had not asked him for the bus which went to the university, this would not have happened."

His father, stony-faced and unforgiving, glared at me on hearing this disclosure. His mother looked at his prone body and sobbed. His fiancée, Neha, looked ashen.

"Why did he go to the theatre alone?" asked the policeman, whipping out his diary. "Did he appear to be disturbed?"

"It's my fault," his father's voice faltered. "We had an argument this morning. I was angry with him because he had given up his bank job to take part in a music reality show."

"I fought with him this morning," sobbed his mother. "I wanted him to get married immediately and settle down."

"It was my fault," said Neha in a low voice. "Once he had given up his job, I had second thoughts about our marriage. Today I told him I wanted to be free."

Everyone turned to look at her, shocked at her confession. Had Neha's decision broken Nikhil completely? Was that why he was in the cinema hall all by himself? Was he trying to get over the imminent breakup? Is that why he had stepped onto the middle of the road? Was it a premeditated step on his part? Was I just a catalyst? Or was it, as I had suspected, just an accident, caused by a callous bus driver who had no concern for human life?

"He was manic-depressive," muttered someone standing close to me. "It runs in the family. They have frequent mood swings, with periods of depression and of elation. During their depressive episodes, they can turn suicidal."

I mulled over what he had said. Nikhil had been almost tongue-tied in the theatre. He had not spoken to me at all, although we had sat next to each other for three hours, not counting the two sentences he had spoken to me while getting me the popcorn. Yet, when I had asked him about the bus which would take me to Model Town, he had stood in the middle of the road flapping his hands like a bird when he knew well, like everyone else in Delhi, about buses, especially minibuses and their track record on road safety. Was it really an accident or did Nikhil have a death wish? Did he deliberately step onto the middle of the road in order to tempt fate? Would things have been different if Neha had been with him? How had he taken Neha's rejection? Had he been stoic about it or did he take it badly? Why had Neha changed her mind? Was it only because of his decision to throw away a secure job in order to chase an uncertain future? Or was it because of his manic-depressive behaviour? Was theirs a love match or an arranged one? That would explain how much Nikhil was affected by the breakup. Questions popped in my brain like corn kernels bursting in the microwave, then collapsed and remained unanswered.

I was about to leave Nikhil's house when I heard Neha's mother mutter softly, "It was a good thing they were not married. Otherwise Neha would have been a widow today."

Her words shocked me, but I guessed that for her Neha and her future came before everything else. And in India, the plight of widows was well known. I saw Neha give a sudden sob, saw the shock in her eyes as she rushed inside the bathroom. As I took leave of everyone and slowly walked down the stairs I could hear her retching loudly in the bathroom. My eyes widened as I realised that Neha could well be pregnant. No one knew better than me that marriage was no longer necessary in order to consummate a relationship.

Once I left Nikhil's house I realised how uncertain life was. One could die at any moment. There were strands in

Nikhil's life that I was unable to unravel. I had not known him at all and yet in a way I had been instrumental in his death and the collapse of the world of the people around him. The guilt would haunt me all my life. If only I had not asked him which bus went to Model Town. If only I had not ventured to see *Kabhi Alvida Naa Kehna* alone. If only I had not fought with Prateek. If only I had sat quietly eating a chicken roll and sipping Diet Coke in Prateek's house, none of this would have happened.

Nikhil's life was over and there was nothing I could do to heal the loss of his loved ones. But I could tie the untidy strands of my life together and weave them into a whole. I realised that at 23, I, an MPhil student at the University of Delhi, was old enough to take stock of my life and make my own decisions. I could choose to have a life with Prateek or without him. I could choose to sanctify my relationship with Prateek and savour the security that marriage would bring. Or I could choose to break free. It was time I came to a decision. I picked up my phone and dialled.

# Betrayal

"Oh hell, the lights have failed again," she muttered to herself as she stood at the doorway. No wonder the doorbell did not ring. She thanked God she was always well prepared for every eventuality during her trips.

She took out the pencil-light torch from her purse and shone it into her bag. Something glittered inside it. The silver keychain. She took the key from her bag, pulled the door towards her, put the key into the lock and twisted it ever so lightly. The door opened noiselessly. She stepped inside, pushing the strolley bag in front of her and then turned back to bolt the door.

Delhi was safe no more. She did not relish the thought of being found dead, her head caved in by some blunt instrument, only because she had failed to take precautions.

"Prakash," she called, a lilt to her voice, and then hearing no response, decided to surprise him anyway. She walked towards the drawing room, the feeble beam of light from the torch showing her the way. "The battery is down," she thought to herself, as she turned towards the bedroom. "I must remember to purchase it tomorrow." She turned the handle.

The door was locked, which surprised her. Why did her husband, when he was alone in the house, need to lock the bedroom door? She knocked gently on the door but there was no response. She banged the door loudly. "Prakash," she shouted, her voice reaching a crescendo as panic set in.

Terrible visions began to torment her, of Prakash hanging by the fan, having committed suicide, a suicide note splashed over the bedroom wall in his own blood. Prakash with his wrists slashed, blood dripping all over the bedroom floor.

"Control yourself," she said to herself, "calm down. It is only sensible for him to lock the door. He is alone in the house. And one has heard so much of gangs out on the prowl at night."

The door opened a chink. Thank God Prakash was safe.

"Veena?" His face looked bemused. "But you were supposed to return only day after tomorrow."

There was no welcoming smile on his face. No hug. Nothing but this question hanging between them. She could sense the awkwardness.

"You don't seem too happy to see me," she complained.

"It isn't that. It is so unexpected. You always ring up if you change your plans," Prakash muttered.

"Well, this once I decided to surprise you. Anyway, I'll talk to you after I change," she said, walking towards the bathroom. Her nightgown was hanging inside and more than anything else she wanted to change into something light and comfortable. But the bathroom door did not budge.

"What's going on, Prakash?" she asked suspiciously. "Just what is going on?"

"Nothing," he said, "let's go to the drawing room and let us chat."

It was quite difficult to see his expression in the dark. Fortuitously the lights came on just then. They flooded the room with light. She banged on the bathroom door once again. After what seemed like ages it opened and Mita came out.

She had forgotten all about her friend Mita, who had arrived two days before her tour, looking for a place to stay.

"I didn't know you would be away," Mita had said, when she had learnt of Veena's impending trip.

"It doesn't matter; you can stay here. I'll be back in a week's time anyway," Veena had said in her usual impulsive way, seeing that her friend was desperate for a place to stay.

Veena suddenly slumped on the sofa. "I wish," she said, "that I had come the day after tomorrow instead."

"I'm sorry," Mita muttered, "I'm really sorry."

As if, thought Veena, the word "sorry" could wash away everything. She felt sickened seeing Mita wearing her nightdress. "I'm moving into the guest room for the night; excuse me," she told Prakash.

Entering the room, she first locked up the room carefully. She then washed her face in the bathroom washbasin. Then she wondered what to do. "I had thought Prakash would rustle up a snack for me," she thought, hunger beginning to gnaw at her. She opened the door and went to the fridge in the dining room. It was empty. "What did Mita and Prakash live on," she wondered nastily, "love and fresh air?"

She cut slivers of cheese, added a slice of pickle, lay it between two slices of bread, put it on a tray along with a can of Diet Coke, and carried it back to her room before locking it carefully behind her.

"Veena." Prakash's knock at the door was desperate.

But she did not want to talk to him. Not today, when she was tired and in shock. "Go away," she shouted. After switching off the lights she tried to fall asleep.

She was surprised when she woke up after a long and undisturbed sleep. It was fatigue, no doubt, that had enabled her to sleep for eight hours at a stretch. The next morning Prakash and Mita were both at her door. She knew she had to face them sometime.

"Let us go into the drawing room," she said, leading the way. As she entered the room, she realised that the previous night Prakash had had the grace to sleep there. The bed sheet lay rumpled on the floor, and she could see the indentation marks of his head on the cushion. Once she may have felt a wave of affection, of desire for him, but now she felt nothing. If at all, she felt a sense of deep revulsion.

"Veena, I can explain," said Mita.

"I know Prakash is attractive," said Veena, "but Mita, a one-night stand?"

"It was not that," Mita bristled. "We actually care for each other."

"Is that true?" she asked Prakash, her voice suddenly becoming very quiet. "Is that true?" she repeated.

For a moment there was pin-drop silence. Much depended on his answer. The fate of three lives hung on balance.

"Well," he stammered, "in a way, yes."

Veena suddenly expelled her breath. The tension was over. Prakash's reply had made her decision easy.

"In that case," she said solemnly, "I will move out of your lives now."

Prakash could hardly believe he had heard her right. "We have been married for seven years. You cannot let this one affair come in the way of our marriage."

"Affair." She laughed shakily. "Mita said you cared for each other, and you agreed; I don't want to come in the way of your happiness. I'll send you the divorce papers."

"You can't do this to me," Prakash gritted his teeth, while Mita looked shocked by the sudden turn of events.

The divorce papers were signed at last. Veena smiled once it was done. The first hurdle was over, and within a few months, the freedom she yearned for would be hers. A freedom which was well earned, she reminded herself. She had known of Prakash's affairs and infidelity for years. But she had not confronted him because she had no proof. All these years she had hoped he would change. He hadn't. Besides his infidelity, she had also borne the brunt of his bouts of bad temper. But she had not let anyone see the cracks within their marriage, no relation, no friend, not even Mita, because she knew that Prakash would never release her. He found his marriage too convenient.

When her patience had been exhausted, Veena had hired a private detective. But Prakash had been too smart. The detective had failed to get any tangible proof against him. She had been reconciled to the thought that her freedom from this loveless marriage would elude her.

And then Mita had arrived. Veena had seen Mita eye Prakash. She knew that look. More importantly, she knew Mita. She wanted Prakash, because he was attractive, because he was unavailable, and most importantly, because he belonged to Veena. She knew Mita. She had known her for years. She knew Mita was relentless in pursuit.

That is why Veena had changed her travel plans. She had hoped to catch them red-handed and she had succeeded. The rest had been easy. She had gambled on the fact that even Prakash would have the grace to say that his affair with Mita was more than a one-night stand. Even if he hadn't, Veena thought resolutely, she had substantial evidence for divorce. But now it would be a divorce by mutual consent and hence less acrimonious. And there was a bonus as well. Mita would marry him, and live with Prakash's affairs and towering rages.

Mita would deserve it. Mita and Prakash were made for each other. Veena gave a sigh of relief. The prospect of freedom suddenly smelt sweet.

# Sleight of Hand

"It's just a sleight of hand," explained the Mastermind, his hands shuffling the deck of cards deftly, while he produced three aces. "The trick is to focus the audience's attention to something else while you perform your trick. As in cards, so also in life."

The words came back to Munna as he stood at the entrance of the Sunday Bazaar, wonderstruck as always, by the spectacular Red Fort on one side of the road and the majestic Jama Masjid on the other. The Red Fort always transported him into another world—the world of emperors resplendent in their magnificent robes, holding a durbar, of the *Diwan-i-Khas* and *Diwan-i-Aam*, of the commoners seeking justice and the emperors dispensing it. He thought of the begums, clad in their finery, strolling down the Red Fort, across the banks of the Yamuna, which used to flow right behind it. He remembered watching the sound-and-light show at the Red Fort, sitting on his father's lap, when he had been but a child.

Life had been so different then. But soon it changed completely. In his dreams he could still see the faces of the three men, leering at him, while knifing his father to death, simply because life in a chawl was always at a discount and a drunken brawl was as good an excuse as any to indulge in violence. There had been no arrests as there had been no witnesses. His mother had forbidden him to say anything to the police. She had bought his silence with one sentence: "You have a young sister at home."

In his dream, Munna stood at the *Diwan-i-Aam* and asked for justice and the emperor in flowing robes dispensed it. Munna thought of his life after his father's death, when he had learnt to use his long legs to take flight. He shook his head, trying to wipe off the voice of his sister screaming,"Munna, run, I say run," urging him, clutching a loaf of bread, to run across the street as fast as his legs could carry him. He had begun to steal, because while hunger had become a way of life since his abba had been killed, even he had been unable to sleep on an empty stomach three nights in a row.

Munna entered the Sunday Bazaar and walked towards the first table of clothes laden with shawls, sweaters, overcoats, and coats, and then went through each of them carefully. Finally he picked up a sweater, put it across his chest as though to try it, discarded it, shrugged his shoulders, surreptitiously slid the briefcase he was carrying under the table, and walked away, hoping the sound of *tick tock, tick tock* coming from inside the briefcase, would remain muffled for some more time.

"Hey you," a voice rang out after him loud and clear, "you left your briefcase behind."

"Drat," thought Munna angrily, "it should not have been discovered so soon; in fact it should not have been discovered at all."

Although the Mastermind had not told him what it contained, he had guessed; he could hear the sound of ticking coming from the briefcase. The Mastermind had not taken him into confidence. He trusted no one. But Munna knew he was part of the plan, a piece of jigsaw in the whole operation. And now, because someone had spotted the briefcase, the whole plan was in jeopardy. Had he not been careful enough? Had his appearance been a dead giveaway? Had he aroused someone's suspicions? What had he been told to do in such an eventuality? Mastermind's voice came back to him: "Carry on regardless. We have a backup plan. We always do. But do not get caught."

Munna carried on, as instructed, not daring to look back, but the voice of the caller only got louder. People began to look curiously at him. He panicked and ran ahead, almost cannoning into a Freida Pinto lookalike, whose face was partly hidden by the armload of flowers she was carrying. As he heard the sound of footsteps coming from behind him, he began running from the Sunday Bazaar towards Chandni Chowk, where the crowds were jostling with each other as well as with rickshaws, push carts, and cows, making speedy movement impossible.

"There is safety in numbers," he told himself, assured by the thought that he would find it easy to lose himself in the sea of humans in Chandni Chowk. But he realised that he had made a mistake. Each step in Chandni Chowk was difficult to take and he was dazed by the dizzying smells of jalebi being fried in pure ghee, of aloo *tikkis* sizzling on a huge tawa, and of cow dung mingled with the fragrance of mogra strands a young urchin was trying to sell. As he jostled his way ahead he found his path blocked unexpectedly by a wayward cow and as he deftly stepped aside to let it pass he was almost knocked down by an incoming rickshaw.

He knew that by this time the police would have been informed by the stall owner and the bomb-defusion squad would have been called. But he was sure that no one would dare to open the unclaimed briefcase before the squad arrived. Secure in that knowledge, with feet flying, Munna Shah, winner of the 800-metres race in high school, raced ahead. He knew the pot-bellied stall owners of the Sunday Bazaar would be no match for him. He remembered what the Mastermind had said when he had recruited him: "You are as swift as a hare; no one can match you. That is why you have been chosen."

He did not dare to look back at his pursuers. He hoped to lose them in the crowd. He knew what the Mastermind had told him, that he had only to reach the end of the road, turn to the by-lane, climb the stairs of the last house, and return to a hero's welcome.

The bullet hit him in the middle of his back. He tripped forward, felled by the tearing pain as well as the burning sensation, saw the blood gushing out and realised that the bullet had pierced his heart. As his eyes began to glaze, he saw the face of the Freida Pinto lookalike gazing at him pityingly.

The bomb blew up in the Sunday Bazaar at the same time—not in the briefcase that had been opened by the bomb-defusion squad and that contained only an innocent alarm clock, but in the bundle of flowers that had been left on the nearby table, while the girl whom nobody remembered had chased Munna. The blast took with it 19 lives, as well as 12 arms, 8 legs and 6 pairs of eyes.

The girl looked at Munna's prone body sadly. The jostling crowd had hardly noticed the fallen boy. No one had seen where the bullet had been fired from; they had no reason to suspect that his death had anything to do with the young girl wrapped up in a red-and-black Naga shawl. He was too young to die, she thought ruefully. And he had no idea that he would die. But it had all been for the Cause. And that justified the Sacrifice. The Cause would always be bigger than the individual. And that is why she was in it.

She walked slowly and confidently to the end of the street, into the by-lane and up the stairs where she knew a rousing welcome awaited her. The Mastermind smiled as he saw her enter the room, rose as though in salutation, and then shot her.

The Mastermind shrugged as he wiped the gun carefully and put it back in the drawer. It was a pity that she had to die, he thought, looking at her beautiful face. She reminded him of someone, he thought, his brows knitted into a frown. The girl whose posters he had seen littered all over the street, from the film *Slumdog Millionaire*.

But it was all for the Cause. And that justified the Sacrifice. It was important to create diversionary tactics, he had told them, to carry off a successful operation. And he had done just that. Munna was the diversion. His own men had shouted after him, so that attention would be drawn to the gangling youth, letting the girl do her task in relative peace. And he had succeeded. He had himself been shaken by the intensity of the blast. It was a pity about Munna and the girl. But the Mastermind was glad that while he had told them about the need for the diversionary tactics, he had wisely not informed them that it was equally important to leave behind no witnesses.

# The Ashes

The night appears haunted. I see the lengthening shadows and stand rooted to the doorstep. Perhaps I am the one who is haunted by the past. The nocturnal silence is deafening. My sense of trepidation grows as I enter the house I had left so abruptly seven years ago.

I remember it all so well, my leaving it raving and ranting, shouting and screaming, all emotion and fury, threatening that I would never return, promising myself that I would never return. It is a promise I have not broken during all these seven years.

But here I am, breaching my promise, back to the house I had abandoned years ago. She is not there, my saintly looking mother-in-law, who had stood at the top of the steps, silent as a sphinx, her eyes gloating, her lips stretched mirthlessly.

I railed at the injustice and the unfairness of it all, my eyes blazing with fury, wondering how a marriage could crumple because a saint-like witch had wished it so, how the vows taken before the sacred fire could crumble so easily, how a man who had promised to love and protect his wife could stand impotent and helpless, weak, spineless and gutless as always, torn between his wife and his mother. I saw Neha, just 16 years old, with a pinched face and terrified eyes, too paralysed to voice her thoughts, but looking at me beseechingly as though telling me not to go.

Maji is not there. She had departed to the other world a year ago.

"To Heaven," Sumit would say.

"Rotting in Hell," I would insist.

It doesn't really matter, as long as the earth is rid of the burden of her existence. There is some justice in this world, after all. The presiding deity of Hans Mahal has gone. The abominable matriarch is no longer there. Instead I see Neha, lurking in the shadows. As she switches on the light on the porch, I see her all too clearly. Her eyes are still too huge for her face. But her face glows. For her sake I hope it is love. She deserves happiness. She has seen so little of it. She comes forward, her steps faltering, her hands by her sides. I open my arms and hug her to my bosom. My child, my daughter, my life.

She carries my little strolley bag into the house. The bag speaks volumes. It makes it abundantly clear that my visit does not herald the return of the daughter-in-law. I am just a guest who has been called to attend her daughter's wedding. I shall return once the wedding is over. Sumit will have to put up with me for a week—that is all.

Neha clears her throat. I can smell trouble. "Ma," she says, "my friends and I are partying tonight."

"I understand," I say. But I don't. I do not understand why my daughter wants to spend time with her friends when she should be spending it catching up with her mother. But I realise that seven years is a long time. It has taught Neha to live without her mother. And FaceTime on an iPad is not a substitute for my physical presence. I should not have left without my daughter. I should have fought for her, consequences be damned. I knew that Sumit would not seek a divorce. Not yet. Not until Neha was married. It is always difficult to marry off a daughter from a broken home. The façade has to be maintained. Hence, the return for the prodigal daughter-in-law.

I hug her and say, "Have a good time."

Sumit enters the drawing room just then. "Thanks for coming," he says gruffly.

"It's only for Neha's sake," I say immediately, drawing the battle lines between us more clearly. There is no coming together. There is no question of setting the clock back. The breach is irrevocable. I see the relief on his face. I have made it abundantly clear that I have no expectations from him.

He clears his throat. "I am going to the club," he says. He has found his escape. I am unwanted. Sumit could not have said it more clearly in words.

The maid takes me to my room and opens the door. I enter and give a cursory glance to the room that I had left so abruptly seven years ago. Nothing seems to have changed. There is a damp patch on the ceiling. The bathroom upstairs must be leaking. It appears as though Sumit had locked my room when I left and it has remained untouched. The bed has a familiar blue bedspread on it. Silk, Fabindia—my favourite. The fan is gleaming. The mahogany table stands polished.

The maid lights a fire in the grate.

"If I close the windows and sleep," I joke, "I will surely die of carbon monoxide poisoning."

The maid looks blankly at me for a moment. Then I notice something new.

It stands on the mantelpiece—a small copper container, with a red sacred thread tied around it, gleaming and shining, staring unblinkingly at me. Just the ideal container to soak the dry sticks of *chirata* I have brought with me, my own home remedy to battle prediabetes.

The window is partially open. I wonder which idiot did that. Perhaps the maid took my remark about carbon monoxide seriously. I shut the window and wrap my sweater tightly around myself. I hate the cold. I hate it morbidly, as though it is not just the weather but a mortal enemy.

The wind bites into my skin and I can feel my fingers begin to throb with pain. My knuckles turn red and painful. I do not need to wait for the doctor's report to confirm the diagnosis. I know that it is the beginning of rheumatoid arthritis, which I must have inherited from my mother. I look with morbid fascination at my hands. Hands that Sumit had once admired, held tightly, kissing the fingers one by one. Hands that books have classified as artistic.

And I am an artist. I teach Art in Mirambika in Delhi. I have done so for the last seven years. I have begun holding exhibitions in art galleries. My first solo exhibition took place two months ago. I am not an M.F. Hussain. But I am slowly making a name for myself.

But it will all come to an end, slowly and painfully, as it had for my mother, unless there is a miracle cure. Unless stem cells can perform some miracle. I smile. I have begun anticipating the worst even before it is diagnosed. That is my defence mechanism at work. If I anticipate it, it will not appear to be so bad once the blow falls, if at all it does fall. I have not come to Shimla to treat my aches and pains or more serious ailments. I have come to attend my daughter's wedding.

My father-in-law is upstairs. He is bedridden. I must go and see him. I walk into his room and see him lying shrivelled up, a virtual skeleton, all skin and bones. An attendant sits by his side, looking moronic, a beatific expression on her bovine face. I bend down and touch my father-in-law's feet. I can see his eyes following me. I think I can see a glimmer of a smile on his face, but I know it is my overwrought imagination at work. I sit on the straight-back chair and wonder what the mandatory time one must spend before one can leave a patient is. "Five minutes," I decide. I leave after that time, walking down the wooden staircase, my feet leaden.

At 7 pm I begin to feel hungry. The maid comes to the room with a glass of milk and some biscuits. I am too proud to ask her for something more.

"Dinner," she says, "is at 9.30."

But Neha is partying with friends and Sumit has gone to the club, where he will drink until his friends carry him back in an almost comatose state into his car. Subhash, the driver, will bring him home and put him in bed. Sumit is very predictable. He doesn't change. He has a drinking problem, which we have all tried to ignore. The scion of an old aristocratic family in Shimla will not admit to being an alcoholic. It is simply not done. I wonder at the state of his liver. But that is his problem; it is no longer mine.

I will be eating dinner alone, I realise. Two-and-a-half hours is a long time. My stomach growls. I wait for the maid to leave and then open the chicken biryani I had brought along with me, packed and sealed in aluminium foil, which I had planned to devour on my journey before entering the sanctified, hallowed portals of this hellhole. It has turned cold. I grab the thali, pour the chicken biryani in it and stand for a few minutes before the fire before I begin eating. Chew, chew, gnaw, gnaw, my teeth in perfect harmony, like a rat's, tearing into the chicken. I grind the flesh, savouring every morsel. It is not just the chicken I tear into but much more, memories, insults, and people dead and gone.

The windows of my room begin to rattle. I suspect that a storm is in the offing. I shiver. It begins to rain. It was raining that night when I was returning from Delhi to Shimla after attending a niece's wedding. Rain had lashed on the AC first class compartment's window. I had shivered on the lower berth as the train passed through the tunnels, all 101 of them. The next day Maji with her prim lips and piercing eyes told Sumit, "Snigdha spent the night alone with Paarth."

I blanched on hearing her. "We merely travelled together in the train," I clarified.

"In the AC first class coupe," she said slowly, emphasising every word.

Sumit's eyes darkened. "Is that true?" he had asked.

"Yes," I admitted, "but I had nothing to do with it. It was not a rendezvous. Your agent had booked my return tickets."

Sumit was nonplussed. He knew I was speaking the truth. Then he saw Maji looking meaningfully at my arms and my midriff. He could see the faint purple bruises on them. My skin bruised easily. He flung my pallu away and saw the marks on my midriff, shoulders and arms.

"Listen, Sumit, let me explain," I had said.

But he was in no mood to listen. He slapped me hard across the face, not once, not twice, but thrice, and then choked me, leaving me gasping for breath. I found him pressing my windpipe and my eyes began to bulge. I then kicked him in the shin, which made him loosen his hold on me, and then shouting and screaming, raving and ranting, I left, raging against the unfairness of it all, promising never to return even as Maji smiled her enigmatic Mona Lisa smile and saw me leave.

My revenge, I swore to myself, would be when I turned her allegation into a reality. When I opened my doors and my arms to Paarth, when I let my body do all the speaking. When I had a man, and not a drunken lout, make love to me, making me feel like a complete woman. But I was tied up in knots by my middle-class morality and could not reveal the horror of Sumit's allegations to Paarth, who was also a teacher in my school at Shimla. For whom I had yearned all these years whenever we met each other.

I remembered travelling in the coupe with him and my heart hammering loudly in my chest. Hope, anticipation or trepidation, I do not know which emotion dominated me. I had seen his eyes follow me when he had come to Hans Mahal. I had spent 10 years in the same school as him. I remembered the physical ache that accompanied the yearning I felt as I balled my hand into fists and tried to sleep. I wished he had the guts to take me. I had yearned for him and moaned softly while he had stayed still on the upper berth. I had whispered his name under my breath, hoping that he would hear, but he hadn't. I closed my eyes and imagined that he was on top of me, making love to me with wild abandon. I dug my hands into my flesh, on my arms and on my midriff, pretending that it was him. The train had gained momentum and rushed forward, rattling loudly through the pitch-dark tunnel, chugging along. I thought of Paarth, whom I would have liked to have held and hugged and kissed and loved, but who lay stiff and wide-eyed, bound by rules of morality far stricter than mine, even when the train passed through tunnel after tunnel, when the compartment seemed charcoal-black and pitch-dark. When my flesh had yearned for him and I had wanted to scream.

I cried against the unfairness of it all. For being accused of a crime I had wanted to commit, but had not committed. Feeling ashamed to admit that the bruises were self-inflicted because I had lusted after a man who was not my husband, so that once, just once, I would be treated like a woman and not a cadaver. Perhaps Maji, with her beady little eyes, had seen the yearning in my face whenever Paarth came to our house. Her hawk-like gaze missed nothing.

My recollections make me restless. I begin to feel thirsty. I need a glass for drinking water. But I do not want the maid to come and see me devour chicken in a household that is pure vegetarian. I spy the brass container. Perhaps I can fill it with water and drink. I open the container. My arthritic fingers bend and I drop it right into my plate. Ashes fall into it. An urn—that is what it is. It contains the mortal remains of someone. Everything falls into place immediately. I gaze with horror at the grey-white ashes. I can guess what they are. Ashes of my mother-in-law. Nestled peacefully on the mantelpiece, waiting for her husband to die so that she can be united with him.

Snatches of what she had once told me come back to me, that in their family when a wife dies her ashes are kept till her husband passes away. Then her ashes along with his are scattered in the Ganga.

"Ugh!" I had said. "How can one be confined in a tiny urn for years to come? What if the husband outlives his wife by 20 years?"

Her eyes had blazed as she had said, "A woman has no existence apart from her husband." Her eyes were expressive. And in this house her word was law. I could only hope that, my Karva Chauth fasts notwithstanding, I would outlive my drunken husband.

Maji had died last year. I had not been called for her *chautha*. I would not have been called for Neha's wedding but for the fact that Sumit must have pretended that it was work and not anger that had taken me away. Hence the invitation card. Hence the summons. Hence my presence in the house I had sworn never to enter when I had left it.

Neha is getting married after a week. Who is the boy? I forgot to ask her that. I hope for her sake that his mother is dead so that he is not tied to his mother's apron strings. All men are mama's boys. The placental cord never gets cut, at least metaphorically, until the mother dies.

My nerveless fingers shake. I do not know how to control them. I am a spastic child, with no control over my limbs. I ball my hands into fists. I cannot confess that I had dropped the urn to Sumit. I know Sumit. I know what he is capable of doing. I cannot tell him that his mother's mortal remains are mingled with chicken biryani. I wonder what will happen if Sumit finds out. Will he coil his short and stubby fingers around my neck and try to choke me as he had done the last time, when he wanted to know the truth about Paarth and me?

I do not know what to do. An empty urn will rouse suspicion. Thank God the matchbox is still there. As I said, nothing has changed in the room except for the addition of the little brass container. I take a copy of the magazine that covered my art exhibition in detail.

It's a sacrifice. I had wanted to show the magazine to Neha. But I have no choice. Inside the bathroom I switch on the light, tear the magazine into shreds and burn it. I see the paper burn into black ashes and scatter on the floor. It doesn't resemble the ashes in the urn in the least. I then switch on the exhaust fan to drive out the smoke. I do not want anyone to smell the acrid stench. Otherwise Sumit will wonder whether I am burning Parth's letters. I know how his narrow and stupid mind works.

I have a plan. That night I stoke ashes in the grate and take out a handful. I touch the charcoal with my hand and almost yelp with pain. The ashes are still hot. But I know that a blast of cold air will cool them. I open the window slightly and cold air gushes in. Fifteen minutes later the ashes are cold.

I mix the ashes with the burnt-up paper. I look at the blend of whitish grey ashes and blackened burnt paper in consternation. They do not really resemble the ashes that had fallen from the urn. But they will have to do. I am all for authenticity, but here it is a question of my survival. I scoop them up on a sheet of paper and pour them into the urn. I have covered nearly half the urn.

I return the remnants of the chicken biryani mingled with Maji's ashes into the Ziploc bag I had carried. After midnight, I creep into the kitchen and bury it deep into the black bin bag. I know Sumit and Neha will not wake up. Both are heavy sleepers. Dadaji is bedridden and partially deaf, anyway. In case I am caught, I can claim that I had entered the kitchen because I am a nocturnal eater or that I wanted to make myself a cup of tea.

On my return to my room I keep the urn back on the mantelpiece. I wish my father-in-law a long life. I wish he lives to be a hundred years. But I have seen him grow frail before my eyes. And now he is completely bedridden. I know that he may not last more than two or three summers and even here I am being overly optimistic. I wish, when the time comes for him to leave this world, his end will be painless. I know Sumit will go to Garh Mukteshwar, Prayag, Haridwar or Gaya for dispersing the ashes of his parents into the Holy Ganga.

Knowing him, Sumit will not look into the urn as it will make him distinctly queasy. I imagine him in Haridwar, talking to the priests, negotiating with them like the bania he is at heart. I can imagine him making an elaborate list of the items required for the puja. I can see him taking a morning bath at 5 am, shivering slightly in the cold. I can imagine him wearing a dhoti, holding his stomach in so that it does not protrude, and performing the puja. I can see him going by boat and scattering the ashes in the Ganga, praying that his parents are at peace, now that they are at one with the elements. I know that he will merely open the urn and tip the entire lot into the Ganga. And even if he sees the ashes and is surprised he will not blame me for the way his mother has disintegrated.

In the meanwhile, her mortal remains stuck to the biryani will be tipped into the dump. Maybe scavenging dogs will come and tear into the biryani, salivate and lick and devour the uneaten pieces of chicken. Maybe parts of the mortal remains of my mother-in-law will nestle in the stomach of a scavenging dog. My mother-in-law, who said, "*Ladki hui*," when Neha was born, and turned away as though it was a crime to produce a daughter, and who never forgave me or failed to remind Sumit of the fact that after Neha, I was unable to bear another child. My mother-in-law, who urged me to rest just when Sumit was about to return from work, so that he would find his wife asleep in bed while his poor aged mother toiled in the kitchen; who created chasms where bridges should have been built, who drove me out of my own house while pretending to be a bystander.

Inadvertent though it is, I have finally got my revenge.

# The Ideologue

Things have gone terribly wrong. The acrid stench of smoke is all around me. A blanket of smog has enveloped us. I can smell petrol. It is a smell I love, but not when it is splashed on human bodies. How did this happen? Who is responsible?

Was it just two days ago that I was standing here, in the cricket ground inside Delhi University, making an impassioned plea against the proposed reservations? The ground was packed with students. I could see television cameras scattered all around the field. Everyone loves a tamasha. "Down with reservations," I had said, my voice hoarse from shouting. "Down with mediocracy, up with meritocracy."

The slogan sounded nice. I liked the cadence of the words. "Down with reservations," chanted the others. My sentiments resonated with the crowd that stood in the sun, ready to commit itself to a cause.

"21 years ago," I began, my voice passionate, "there was a country-wide agitation against reservations."

There was silence as the students looked avidly at me.

"Rajiv Goswami and many other students agitated against the Mandal Commission Report and sacrificed their lives for it.

"The time has come to agitate once again, to sacrifice if we need to, as they had done, to make the government see reason. We cannot continue to live in a stratified society. In the beginning there were reservations for SCs and STs; after the Mandal Commission there were reservations for the OBCs, and now separate reservations for women have been proposed. The supreme court has been approached for enhancing the ceiling for reservations from 50% to 70%. I would like to ask the government, what about the general category males? What is our crime? Are we children of a lesser god? Will the doors of the prestigious civil services, medical colleges and engineering colleges be closed to us forever? What about our dreams, our hopes and aspirations?" I spoke in clichés, I knew, but it appealed to my audience.

As I spoke about the proposed stratification of society on gender lines, which would have repercussions both at home and at the workplace, my voice was strident, my demeanour uncompromising, and every person hearing me knew that I meant business. I ended my speech with the threat of going on an indefinite hunger strike. The applause that followed my speech did not die down for many minutes.

I must make it clear that I am not a misogynist; nor am I a male chauvinist. Far from it. I respect women. I come from a family of strong women. I know that they can compete with men and excel in all the fields like science, humanities, medicine and engineering. Women have claimed equality with men. By providing them with reservations, the government will do them a disservice. People will lose respect for them, thinking that all women, even those who qualified on merit, came through the quota system. I am not the only one who believes that. Many women agree with me. That is why there were a sizeable number of girls in the university grounds, listening avidly to my speech.

My voice had begun to rise as I was speaking, and I realised that I was emotionally distraught. But I knew I had stirred passions, and whipped up enthusiasm among the crowd of students who had initially been passive. As I sat down, I felt a bit dizzy and emotionally drained. The media had lapped up every word of what I had said. So had the students. I hoped I would get good media coverage.

But this was no time for self-praise. It was time to turn my talk into action. As I sat discussing the strategy with my friends, I decided that the next morning I would begin my fast. I had suggested a hunger strike. Somewhere in-between, the plans had changed to an indefinite fast, somewhat like Anna Hazare's, whose fast at the Jantar Mantar was fresh in the minds of people.

Sumit's was the voice of caution. He had said, "Don't be hasty in suggesting this, Vineet; such decisions take time." Was it he who had spoken exasperatedly, when I had remained adamant about going on a hunger strike?

"You are no Gandhiji who sits on a fast unto death and brings the government to its knees, or even an Anna Hazare whose fast calls for mediation. You are just a mediocre student who has pretensions of being a youth leader." Sumit did not speak these words aloud, but I could see the scorn on his face. "Besides, you will not be able to keep a fast for many days; you love your chicken tikka and beer too much," he said.

My idea of a mass hunger strike was transformed into a one-man indefinite fast, but I did not object to the idea; I thought maybe this would provide me with a national stature. From being a mere student union president, I would be catapulted into national politics.

Protest is in my blood, I admit. In 1949 my maternal grandmother languished in jail for six months under the Preventive Detention Act. But those were heady days, Nani says nostalgically. She talks of Gandhiji and Netaji Subhash Chandra Bose in the same breath. One gave a clarion call for Quit India and the other raised the Indian National Army to oust the British from India. Netaji's slogan, "Give me blood, and I shall give you freedom", scribbled by him in her autograph book, is still cherished by her. There is a catch in her voice when she speaks of these national leaders, who have left such an indelible impression on her mind.

Ma too was in jail between 1975 and 1977, during the turbulent years of the Emergency. Was she moved by idealism or merely the romanticism of protest? Was she an ardent advocate of freedom and liberty, which were curbed during the Emergency, or was she a blind follower of the student leaders of that time? I know that the period during the Emergency was pretty draconian. Ma is tight-lipped about her time in prison. While many of the student leaders of her time are now into national politics, she has remained in oblivion. For her, the prison was a nightmare she would prefer to forget.

"This is a rehearsal for the future," Sumit's voice intruded into my thoughts. I looked at him suspiciously. Did he guess that I had political ambitions of being the chief minister of Delhi one day? Or at least a union minister? But that time was too far away. In politics as in life, one must live one day at a time.

The first two days of the fast went well enough. I felt the hunger pangs but the adulation of the crowds gave me a new high. On the third day I had a dizzy spell. The physician who attended to me diagnosed low blood sugar and dehydration. He ordered me to give up my fast. I had to do something drastic. It was then that I said, "If the government does not accede to our demands, I shall self-immolate myself."

Why did I say that? I do not know. Was I merely aping Rajiv Goswami, who led the anti-Mandal agitation? Did I have a death wish? Why did I not notice the news reporter lurking in our midst? Why did the news channel pick up my threat and flash it at regular intervals? Wasn't there any national news worth airing? But the deed was done. I was trapped by my own words. To back down would have been cowardly. I would have lost face among the student community. A student leader must stand tall.

That evening as we sat discussing our future strategy, I could see Aarti looking worriedly at me. Aarti hates violence. She is a pacifist, a Gandhian in her beliefs. The world of realpolitik is not for her. She knew that my threat to self-immolate could lead to large-scale violence.

I caught the yearning look Sumit gave Aarti. "This is what is called 'dog-like' devotion," I thought mirthlessly. I should have felt sorry for Sumit. Once he and Aarti were a couple, until I snatched her away from him. But I was not sorry. Everything is fair in love and war, I said to myself. Only I had realised that it was not love. I was becoming tired of her, as I had of the others before her. The thrill was in the chase, and the conquest, and in this case, taking away from Sumit what he coveted. But once she was mine, my interest in her began to dwindle. My heart had already begun to wander.

I prayed that the government would defer bringing in the legislation proposing reservations, now that the media was playing up my threat of self-immolation. But I knew that it was merely wishful thinking on my part. The general elections were scarcely a year away. The government would bring in the legislation immediately to win over half the electorate. And no political party would dare to oppose the reservations. It was such an emotive issue.

For me it was a do or die situation. I had no choice but to act upon my threat. I tried hard to find a way out. And finally I hit upon a solution. That evening I had my plan ready. I instructed Sumit to get two water balloons filled with kerosene. I planned to place them in the armpits of my kurta. At the right moment I would prick the balloons and the kerosene would spill down my kurta. I requested Sumit and my other friends to create a diversion so that the attention of the police was drawn away from me. I would then drop my lighted cigarette on my pyjamas, which would catch fire. Before the police could react, the deed would be done.

"Just keep a few buckets of water ready to douse the flames before I am seriously hurt," I said and winked at Sumit. I knew he would do my bidding. He had been doing it for years. The water would not rouse suspicion either. My friends would claim that it was meant for drinking. I reached the university grounds early the next morning. A number of policemen had been deployed there. The government was expecting me to carry out my threat of self-immolation. I continued with my fast before the anxious crowd. The police were on the lookout for my supporters carrying cans of kerosene. Suddenly there was a loud altercation between two men. The fight turned into an ugly brawl. The attention of the police was diverted towards them as they swooped upon the two and pulled them apart, threatening to arrest them for disturbing the peace. A minute was all I needed to jab the balloons, and then light a cigarette and touch my pyjamas, which went up in flames. I could smell petrol and burning flesh.

"Water! Water!" I shouted. This was no time for heroics. I did not wish to die like this. I saw just one bucket of water nearby. Where were the other buckets of water I had asked for? As Sumit hurried towards me, he tripped and knocked over the bucket and the water splashed on the ground. He did the next best thing. He rolled me on the floor to douse the flames.

Something has gone wrong—very wrong. Sumit's face is white. He calls a friend for help. They roll me on the floor repeatedly. I can see the blisters on Sumit's hands. They will hurt like hell for months. "Call the ambulance," I gasp. I have never suffered such agony before. My entire skin seems to have peeled off. I wish someone could give me morphine, to lessen my pain. I wonder if I will survive until the ambulance comes. I wonder what burn victims die of. Injury? Septicaemia? Or something else?

The ambulance arrives at last. "Safdarjung Hospital Burns Unit," says Sumit. The words are etched in my mind. My flesh continues to hurt. I still feel like I am on fire. I think of the boys and girls who died during the anti-Mandal agitation in 1990. What inspired them to sacrifice their lives? Were they courageous or merely foolhardy? And what was the fine dividing line separating the two?

I have no claim to martyrdom. I am not cut out for heroics. I am a victim of a plan gone awry. I look at my burnt hands and misshapen fingers. What percentage of burns have I suffered? Will I be able to play the guitar? More importantly, will I live? Agitations recede into the background. Now I am fighting for my survival. Do I really care if there is 20% reservation for women? Today I would happily advocate the proposed reservations, if only I could put the clock back. Why did I not listen to Sumit when there was still time?

The ambulance stops in Safdarjung Hospital and I am wheeled on the stretcher inside the Burns Unit. I remember little after that. Everything is a blur. I remember little of the attending doctors and what they have to say about me. I suspect I may have passed out for a few minutes. When

I open my eyes I find myself in a room. For a moment I wonder where I am. I am totally disoriented. Then I see Sumit standing outside the door, talking to the doctor. I hear the doctor say, "70% burns, most of them in the upper torso. There is a danger of septicaemia. The chances of survival are low." He is not talking to me. He does not care if I can hear him. For him, I do not exist. I am already a cadaver. Only my date of departure from this world is not certain. He has given up on me, as has everyone else.

Sumit enters the room, a mask covering his mouth, taking precautions that he does not infect me. Though his mouth is covered, his eyes are smiling. How can he smile when I am about to die? He looks at me sardonically. Or maybe I am overwrought and am imagining things.

Then I remember something. There being just one bucket of water instead of the many buckets I had asked for. Sumit knocking down the bucket of water, which would have reduced the intensity of my burns. Sumit rolling me on the floor, the way burns were treated in the olden days, making the burns go much deeper. The petrol in the balloons instead of kerosene. That could not have been a mistake.

My conviction grows. In the midst of my pain and discomfort I can only mouth one word. "Why?"

Sumit looks at me intently. He has no difficulty in understanding what I am trying to ask.

In a flash I understand why he did it. Aarti.

"All's fair in love and war," he says. "There are many ways of protesting against injustice. You chose yours. I chose mine."

# Alms and the Woman

It is a working mother's worst nightmare. As I stand at the entrance door and wait for Ruhi to open it, I wonder what is taking her so long. Perhaps she is in the bathroom, I tell myself. I open the door with my key and enter. The house seems empty. My throat is dry, as are my lips. As usual, I expect the worst. "Ayesha, Ayesha," I say, as I move from room to room, waiting for a miracle to happen, waiting to see my baby sleeping in her cot, or gurgling and cooing, as is her wont. But today there is just silence.

There is no sign of Ruhi or Ayesha. The girl from Jharkhand, whom I had trusted with my daughter, has fled. I begin trembling. My body starts shaking. I try to shout, to call out Ayesha's name, but instead I begin to choke. I feel a sudden pain in my chest and start sweating profusely. If I didn't know any better, I would think this was the onset of a heart attack. But I know what it is—a panic attack. Keep calm, I tell myself, do not think the worst. There must be a simple explanation for it. But my anxious, overwrought mind cannot think of anything. There is nothing more I want to do than bawl. But I force myself to breathe deeply. "Stay calm, stay calm," I tell myself repeatedly. If Ruhi has indeed disappeared with Ayesha, I need to contact the police. And for that, I must stay calm. I delve into my purse, pop a pill in my mouth and swallow it with a sip of water. I continue to take deep breaths and slowly the pain in my chest subsides.

I then hear footsteps climbing up the stairs. A key turns into the door and I see Ruhi with Ayesha in her arms. "Ruhi," I shout, unable to restrain myself, "I thought you had taken Ayesha and disappeared! I thought I had lost Ayesha."

Ruhi stands still. She doesn't defend herself against my allegations. "I am sorry, Didi," she says, "but you never come home before lunch."

Both she and I know that I am never home before 2 pm and right now it is just 1 pm. She chides me gently. "Didi, what were you afraid of? Why would I walk away with your daughter? If I wanted to, wouldn't I steal your son instead?"

Her words begin to make sense. I flush guiltily. I admit that I tend to overreact. And lately I have been prone to panic attacks, for which I have consulted a psychiatrist. I was not always like this. But I have not been myself ever since Manu walked out of our lives. Or rather, ever since I surprised him in one of his "closed-door meetings" with his clients, only to find him entwined so closely with a business associate that it took him a good five minutes to realise that I had entered his room. He tried to laugh it off, and to mock my puritanical mindset, but I took it seriously and walked out of the marriage with my children in tow. Since then I had been trying to live by myself, and living alone was tough. Being a single mother was tougher. But I had no one to turn to. Not my brother Rajnish, who lived in Tunisia, nor my widowed mother, who had warned me eight years ago that I was making a terrible mistake by marrying Manu—a mistake I would live to regret.

I sat down on the sofa with a thump. Although I had taken maternity leave, I wished that I could take childcare leave, to look after Ayesha. I wish I had not spent all two years of the childcare leave, which, after the Sixth Pay Commission, the Government of India so generously offered, so I could be with my son. But Arnav had been a dream come true. I could never have enough of him. I wanted to be there for him, when he first sat up, when he first rolled off the bed, when he took his first baby steps. I never thought I would have another child.

"The mistake," Manu had laughed, when I conceived Ayesha. I had flinched on hearing him. He could not have made it clearer that the new baby was not welcome. I had walked away from him soon after Ayesha was born, with little more than my tattered pride.

"There is nothing a hot cup of coffee will not cure, Didi," says Ruhi. She has a solution to all my problems. I always thought the English said a pot of tea was the panacea for all ills. But Ruhi knows better. And her cup of coffee does invigorate me. After putting Ayesha to bed, she enters the kitchen to make coffee. I can close my eyes and imagine her spoon Nescafe Classic into a mug, pour the hot water and milk into it, stirring all the while, and bring it to me. I can almost smell the aroma of the coffee and know that it will provide me instant relief from my headache.

I have an hour before I go back to work, because I had sneaked in from work an hour before the official lunch break. I cuddle up to my little girl for a snooze as Ruhi hurries to the neighbourhood school to bring Arnav back. Ayesha is still suffering from a cold and cough. I am worried. My little girl is prone to infections. It may be because Ruhi has to take Ayesha along with her when she goes to pick Arnav up from school. My thoughts turn towards my son. Does Arnav miss his father? And if so, how much? Ayesha has never known and will never know her father, and she will not miss what she has not known. I see Ruhi looking at me pityingly.

A month later I receive a call from Ma. She springs a surprise on me. She is coming to visit me. I have to receive her from the railway station. "All is forgiven." She has not said as much, but I can read between the lines. She has forgiven me for marrying Mr Wrong. She has also forgiven me for not trying to make my marriage with him work.

"Happy days are here again," I say to myself.

My mother is sheer magic. With her I become a five-year-old. I can rest my head on her shoulder and drop off to sleep. Her visit to Delhi will provide me with a well-deserved reprieve. I will not have to worry about my children.

Perhaps it is the thought of my mother that reminds me of Ayesha. There is nothing more that I want to do than to hold Ayesha before I go to the station. So, en route, I go home. The house is empty once again. For a moment I wonder where Ayesha is. But this time I do not panic; I know that she is safe. I know that Ruhi takes her out for a bit of fresh air before it is time for her to go and fetch Arnav from school.

The railway station is packed with people, even though Nizamuddin is not as busy as the New Delhi station. People jostle with each other on the crowded platform. The smell of sweat permeates the air. My stomach begins to growl. I keep aside my aversion for everything fried with vanaspati oil and dig my teeth into a samosa that comes hot off the *karhai*. There is something to be said for things that are starchy and sinful; they are also satiating. I give a belch of satisfaction, just as the train enters the platform.

I love trains. I have happy memories of train journeys, of travelling for our summer vacations to hill stations like Shimla, Mussoorie, Nainital and Darjeeling. The overnight train journeys helped in bonding the family together and I felt cocooned in their love and warmth. Any sibling rivalry between Rajnish and me was forgotten. But there is no time to ruminate. Ma stands at the entrance of the AC II tier compartment, holding on to the handles on both sides, her back ramrod straight, her face stern—the archetypical matriarch.

I rush towards her compartment and stretch out my hand. She rejects it, gets down, and begins to walk. I hadn't realised how old she has become.

"Arthritis," she says, and I marvel at her ability to read my mind.

We walk towards the exit. Ma has brought just one suitcase, a large Samsonite with a handle and wheels, something I can push with ease while she walks at the even pace that has now become her hallmark.

We step out of the gate and I begin to look for a taxi. Ahead of us, I see women in rags, clutching children in their arms, begging for alms. I feel sorry for them. I am grateful to God that I have a government job and can provide well for my children. I am also thankful for the fact that, by now, Ayesha must be safely tucked in her bed. I know I have to thank Ruhi for this. I am happy she keeps the house so clean. It must be because Ruhi is a Christian, I chuckle to myself. She works for me only because she needs the money to send her children to Don Bosco Public School in Ranchi. She is neat and clean. I see her wearing ironed sarees whenever she goes out. She wears new salwar-kameez suits every now and then. I must be paying her really well, I say to myself, and chuckle some more.

Then I see a woman walking ahead of me. There is something familiar about her gait. I have seen her somewhere. There is also something familiar about the baby she is holding in her arms, even as she is begging for alms. I cannot see the baby clearly. She is covered in a dirty little blanket, but her feet are protruding out. I realise why the baby seems familiar. I recognise the blanket. It is blue, now faded with the passage of time, with footballs in black and white printed on it. It is Arnav's old blanket. I peer at the baby's feet and see a black birthmark below her big toe. Just like Ayesha's. It can't be, I say to myself, as I see the woman wearing a dirt-smeared, greyish black saree walking ahead of me.

But I can restrain myself no longer. I may be making a mistake, but I must be sure. I see a man in a khaki outfit near the gate. Railway Protection Force. I approach him. He listens to me, raises his eyebrows incredulously, and looks at me sneeringly. I thrust my official identity card at his face. He shrugs his shoulders and then walks towards the woman, drops a 10-rupee note in her begging bowl, and as her eyes widen with surprise, he lunges towards the baby and lifts the cover off its face.

Even when it is streaked with grime, I can recognise Ayesha's face anywhere. She is sleeping heavily, unmindful of the world. In normal circumstances I would be happy. But to my eyes she seems to be almost comatose. Just what has Ruhi fed my baby? Opium or some other sleep-inducing medicine? No wonder Ayesha is such a docile, biddable child. No wonder Ruhi is such a well-dressed maid. No wonder Ayesha is so prone to infections; she is exposed to jostling crowds outside the railway station. No wonder I am such a prize idiot.

I cannot speak a single coherent sentence any more. Neither can Ruhi. For different reasons. It is my mother who sees Ayesha, understands what has happened, and takes charge, as she always does.

Just how much money does Ruhi make outside the railway station with Ayesha in her arms? Is it as much as the salary I give her or more? From where has Ruhi got the old clothes in which she dresses Ayesha? Where does she change Ayesha before she brings her home? My mind goes back to the day when I had arrived at home only to find it empty. How glib Ruhi had been and how gullible I was. For how long has this been going on? I want to drop down on the floor and begin crying. But I know I cannot create a scene outside the railway station. I should just be grateful that my baby is alive. I can feel the onset of another panic attack. "Breathe deeply," I say to myself as I fumble inside my purse for my medicine.

The man from RPF has now taken hold of Ruhi, who appears to be wondering whether she should fling herself at my feet and beg for mercy or battle it out. She looks at my face, and sees that I am in no mood to forgive. Her face set in mutinous lines, she straightens her shoulders.

"How will I manage without a maid, from now on?" I wonder. I can get a new maid in a jiffy, because my house has a servant quarter, but how can I trust one? I have a crèche at my workplace, but would a crèche in the neighbourhood be more convenient? A jumble of thoughts jostle through my head. Tears start welling up in my eyes.

Then someone presses my hand. I look up at Ma. Her glance is gentle, as are her words. "Don't worry," she says, "now that I have come home."

# Closure

Someone has put a blight on my sister's happiness. Some faceless, nameless, diabolical monster with his mindless action has snuffed out a young life, which in turn has shattered Shreya's equanimity. I see people crowding around Samar's body, laid out on the floor of his drawing room. People congregate so quickly after a tragedy, like vultures.

The house, which should have resounded with laughter and loud music, reverberates with loud wailing that reaches a crescendo, as Samar's mother cries her heart out. I look at her stricken face and something stirs within me. A feeling of compassion I did not know I was capable of.

The ladies' sangeet slated for tonight is off, as is the wedding. There can be no wedding in Vikram's family for one year. Even I, unfamiliar with rites and rituals, know that. Shreya's eyes are dimmed with tears. I see the young boy lying on the floor, and a wave of anger sears through me. Who was the cruel man who mowed down Samar?

My elder sister's face is taut with grief. I know that she loved Samar, Vikram's younger brother. But she is not thinking just of Samar. I know that in a dark, melancholic way she is remembering the past. She is the unlucky woman who, four years ago, had lost Shantanu, her husband-to-be, and parents-in-law-to-be in a car accident, minutes before they were to reach the marriage venue. The car had crashed, due to the negligence of a drunken truck driver who had turned a blind corner and smashed into it.

It has taken us four years to wipe away Shreya's tears and to blot out from her mind the word *"dayan"*, which Shantanu's grandmother had hurled at her. It had taken a fast-track court three months to indict the truck driver for Shreya to realise that she was not in any way responsible for the accident. The driver had gone on appeal and the matter had been pending in high court. Those years had been traumatic. I had seen Shreya wilt. Her grim unsmiling face was a constant reminder that she had lost Shantanu and was unwilling to give life another chance. Last year she had met Vikram and he had helped to put the past behind her.

Standing in Vikram's sprawling bungalow in New Moti Bagh, I begin to feel dizzy. I slip out on the lawn and pull up a cane chair. The garden is in bloom, but I look unseeingly at the rose bush with crimson roses and the patch of sweet peas. I am tired and my nerves are frayed. I admit that yesterday had been hectic.

I had driven down from Chandigarh at midnight, on a momentary impulse, simply because I wanted to surprise Shreya when I arrived for the sangeet; I had earlier informed her that I would be forced to miss the event. I kept the GPS switched on and found that the drive from Chandigarh to Delhi, in the middle of the night, was a rather daunting experience. I kept a can of Red Bull with me, to help me from dozing off, and put on my favourite music, all the numbers like '*Bheegey Honth Tere*' and '*Beedi Jalai Le*'—songs that Pranav simply hated.

As we neared Delhi, I began to feel drowsy. "Nothing that a cup of Shreya's coffee will not cure," I chuckled to myself.

I was glad I reached Delhi without a mishap. As I drove towards my father's house, I got momentarily diverted when I saw Pranav's number flash on my iPhone, which in my haste I dropped on the car floor. I knew that I would never hear the last of it if I didn't answer Pranav on the first ring. I bent down to pick up the phone. I was slightly breathless when I answered Pranav, and I shuddered slightly when the car brushed against a tree and I heard a branch break. I ignored the thud I had heard when I had picked up the phone. Had I run over a boulder, or hit an animal? I could not know as it was still dark. I waited for Pranav's tirade. It was not long in the coming.

"Just where are you?" he shouted.

I winced. "I am in Delhi," I said tonelessly, hoping that he would realise that I was upset.

But Pranav was unmindful of my feelings. "It is 5 am. Have you been driving from Chandigarh throughout the night, with no thought about your safety? Have you forgotten the Nirbhaya case? Do you have no concern for me? You know how anxious I become. Just how unfeeling can you be? How selfish are you?" He continued in this vein for a few more minutes and then banged down the phone, and I heaved a sigh of relief. The tirade had come to an end. As usual it was all about him and not me. But there was a silver lining. Pranav was furious with me and would not speak to me for the next few days. I could enjoy Shreya's wedding in peace. It sounded like sheer bliss.

Visibility was poor, but I drove ahead, relieved that Pranav's anger was spent. I was in an abusive relationship, I admitted to myself. Then why did I not break off with Pranav? Was it sheer habit, or did I, in some strange warped way, love him? Did I suffer from low self-esteem and think that I deserved it? I really did not know. Relationships were habit-forming. One got used to everything. Even verbal abuse. Was Pranav exhibiting concern for me or control? I was not sure. But as I drove towards Bungalow No. 10, Lodhi Gardens, I realised that I needed to decide whether I wanted to marry Pranav or call it quits.

It was difficult to see in the dark, as the street lights were off. I parked my car on the kerb and, after putting the gear lock, I rang Shreya on her mobile phone, not wanting to wake up the entire household.

Shreya came down the stairs in a trice. "Where did you appear from?" she asked, her eyebrows knitted into a frown.

"Out of the bottle," I said and then saw that my sister, who would once have laughed uproariously, was looking blankly at me. The accident that took Shantanu had marred her in many ways. She had forgotten how to laugh. "Chandigarh," I said gently.

"Chandigarh!" she exclaimed. "Don't you know it is unsafe to drive on Delhi roads at night? Have you forgotten the Nirbhaya incident? What if you had an accident? What if you had been killed?" She might have been Pranav's clone. Except that her concern was only for me.

"Well, here I am in one piece," I said, "but I could do with some coffee."

Shreya smiled widely. In a few minutes she made excellent coffee, and as I sipped the strong brew, I experienced a caffeine rush and thought that I would not be able to sleep, but my frazzled nerves won and I fell asleep almost immediately. I had just dozed off when I was woken up by Shreya, her face ashen as she said, "Shweta, get up immediately; there has been an accident."

"Who, when, where—not Vikram?" I mumbled, still groggy.

It was Samar, Vikram's brother. Mummy and Papa were stone-faced when they heard the news.

We all knew why.

As we drove down to Vikram's house there was silence. Earlier I would take in the surroundings greedily—the majestic Leela Palace Hotel, the drive towards the bungalow, the fountain near the entrance gate and the lawn with roses in bloom. Today I could think of no one but Samar, whom I had met once. Once inside the house, we heard all the details. The boy had gone for a jog, when a vehicle had hit him and fled.

"He is slightly built," says Vikram. "It is possible that the driver did not see him."

"He is 14 years old. Nobody could miss seeing him," puts in Shreya.

"Possibly not at dawn."

"Dawn?" I raise my eyebrows. "What was he doing going jogging at dawn?"

"He was practising for the Delhi Half Marathon. He must have got up and gone for a jog, without telling anyone about it. There was a modern night latch on the main door, which gets locked automatically. No one knew when he left. We learnt about it only when the police rang us up. Thank goodness Samar has his mobile with him. And he has stored Mom's name as Amma." Vikram is still talking of Samar in present tense. It will take some time for us to get used to the fact that Samar is no more.

"Just when did the accident happen?" I ask Vikram.

"Between 4.30 am and 5 am," he says.

"Where?" My heart begins to sink. Vikram's family lives in the posh New Moti Bagh area. His father is a high court judge. "Nehru Park, Vikram, just say it," I mutter to myself.

"Prithviraj Road," says Vikram. "Samar had gone to our grandparents' house. Mummy was busy with the wedding preparations; that's why he was sent there," he answers my unspoken question.

The uneasiness I had felt this since morning turns into horror. Prithviraj Road is not far from Lodhi Gardens. I recall driving near Lodhi Gardens at about 5 am. The thud I heard, while bending down to pick up my phone from the car floor, may have been louder than what I had thought. The cat or dog which I suspected I had hit may have been Samar. I should have got out of the car to look, instead of driving away. Maybe I could have rushed him to a hospital in time. He may have survived. But of course it is possible that it was not Samar at all, but an animal that I had hit. There is no way I can know the truth, I tell myself. The thought offers me no solace. I sit down on a garden chair on the lawns and ruminate.

Suddenly I hear a loud noise and something plonks on the lawn in front of me. It is a peacock. I have never seen a peacock inside a residence in Delhi. It spreads its wings and begins to dance. For a minute I forget Samar. I am engrossed in watching the peacock dance. It seems that it is performing just for me. As suddenly as it came, it flutters its wings and flies away. The dance was just a diversion. It had dragged me away from my dismal thoughts. My attention returns to Samar. This had been his house. It had been his right to enjoy this dance. Maybe he had seen it many times. Samar had his life before him. He had his dreams. Maybe to win a marathon someday. But I had snuffed out his dreams.

There is no way that I can know the truth, I tell myself. Maybe if I take a closer look at the car. When I sneak out of the lawns and look at the car that stands on the kerb, I notice slight reddish brown stains near the door. They weren't there yesterday, I know. I had taken the car for a wash just before I left for Delhi. They may be splashes of mud, I tell myself. Or they may be bloodstains. In my heart I know that they are.

If only I had been more careful while driving. If only I had left Chandigarh at 6 am this morning instead of last night. If only I had not given into an impulse to drive down the night before. If only I had not bent down to pick up my phone. I would then have seen a young boy, jogging on the road. If only I had checked the rear-view mirror to see what I had hit. If only I had not been fatigued and bleary-eyed when I drove near Lodhi Gardens. Maybe it was not my car, but someone else's, I say to myself, clutching at straws.

Two policemen enter Vikram's house to condole the family.

"Why are there no CCTV cameras along the road?" Vikram asks angrily. "Why did no one see him on this route?"

"There are no CCTV cameras on this route, Sir," repeats the policeman, shaking his head. "And it was dawn—too early for people to even go for morning walk."

Except Samar, of course. A postmortem was held in the morning and the doctor put the time of death between 4 am and 5.30 am. Pranav's phone came at 5 am. It fits.

But I cannot tell the truth, or what I perceive to be the truth. It was an accident, I tell myself. My telling the truth will not bring Samar back. Besides, my sister's happiness is at stake. If I confess, I will cause an irrevocable breach in Shreya and Vikram's relationship. Shreya deserves a second chance at happiness. Samar's family will learn to live with the tragedy in time. Although I know that Samar's death will continue to haunt me as long as I live.

I turn and see Samar's mother, dressed in white and standing by the door. Her eyes are bottomless pools of pain. She has lost her child, due to my carelessness. She too deserves closure. Not knowing what happened to her son will torment her throughout her life.

I know what I have to do, whatever the price. What is the punishment for rash and negligent driving? A few years in prison? What is the price of a mother's sorrow? Incalculable. I know Samar's mother deserves closure. So do I. Otherwise I will not be able to live with myself.

I walk up to the police officers and say, "I have a confession to make."

# The Martyr

"Why is Papa wrapped in the national flag, Ma?" asks Mithun plaintively.

"Why do you say that?" I say, wondering if he is being facetious. But he doesn't even know the meaning of "facetious"; he is genuinely perturbed. He has seen the tricolour flying at the Red Fort. He has seen it in movies. But he has never seen it wrapped around a man.

"Is he feeling cold?" he asks.

Now I frown while looking at him. He is definitely being cheeky. But I suppose I am being unnecessarily suspicious. He is just six years old. He does not know the meaning of death. This is the first time he has seen a dead man. His father.

I look at Rajesh closely. The flag is wrapped tightly around him, like a shroud. And that is what it is. His eyes are tightly shut. It is my overwrought imagination. Probably a doctor has shut them. But it makes me feel that he is trying to hide inside the flag.

20 soldiers died at Tangdhar in Kashmir. He was one of them. The world is in sympathy with the dead. So are all Indians. Four extremists came and killed 20 jawans. What were the jawans doing? Were they caught unprepared? Maybe the soldiers had fallen asleep, lost to the world, battling their own demons, each one of them, just as Rajesh was. Just as I am. Each one of us has his own demons to fight. For Rajesh it

was guilt, which was the slow poison that had been corroding his insides for years.

He must have been thinking of that evening seven years ago. He has never been able to forget. Neither have I, however much I have tried.

I look away. The top brass in the military is about to arrive. To pay homage to the dead. Rajesh is one of the martyrs. His photograph will be splashed over the newspapers tomorrow. He deserves it. He is a good man. It is so difficult to think of him in the past tense. I expect that I will continue to talk about him in the present. It will be a long time before I will be able to say "was" whenever I speak of him.

The dam bursts at last. The tears begin to flow. I cry. I howl. A sad and melancholic baying which is disturbing. I am not the stoic wife of an army officer. I am just a scared, wounded, weeping widow. Hands help me to a wooden bench. They pat my shoulders in an attempt to console me. But the tears flow unabated.

I have so much to cry about. But no one knows about it, except Dadi. She knows what I am remembering. Because she is thinking about it, too. I am remembering the day when Rajesh had come to "see me". For Dadi it was a coup of sorts. She had got her friend's grandson, a lieutenant in the army, to come to meet me. And he had come to our house one evening, a reticent man with an enigmatic expression that gave me no clue about what he was thinking, although his eyes were fixed on me. I blushed. Perhaps our two-bedroom house was not the place he could talk to me.

So Dadi suggested that we go to the Buddha Jayanti Park. So, although it had turned dark, we walked to the park, which was not far from my house. I was oblivious to my surroundings, to the profusion of flowers, the overgrown grass and the parrots in flight. I was only conscious of the man walking beside me. We sat on a bench in silence, immersed in our own thoughts. I had no idea what to say to a man I had met just a couple of hours ago, but with whom I would spend a lifetime, in case he said yes. I did not think my views in the matter were of any consequence. I have no idea what he was thinking about, but I was mulling over the strange coincidence that both of us were orphans who were raised by their grandmothers. I looked at him covertly from time to time.

Suddenly I saw a shadow emerge from behind us, which struck Rajesh on his head. Rajesh toppled from the bench and fell. "This is what they mean when they say a man was axed," I thought, just as the man dragged me into the bushes.

Two hours later Rajesh got up from his concussion, his head heavy, his vision blurry, with the realisation that I was missing. He found me near the bushes, bruised, battered and bleeding. He did the only thing he could do. He shook his head a little, as if to clear it, lifted me in his arms, and with sure military strides, the hallmark of a soldier, cradled me in his arms and took me home.

At home I lay on the bed, images of men leering at me, of my flesh being kneaded by human hands, floating in my mind. I understood for the first time the meaning of violence, of sweaty bodies and smelly armpits, of weights being rolled on me and off me, of the pain of possession and even greater, the pain of humiliation, as I was pinned to the ground, reminding me incongruously of Jesus Christ being nailed on the cross.

"Say something, Jayati, say something," said Dadi.

But how could I say anything? I was just reliving the nightmare. And I would continue to do so until I died. Because memories like these never go away. They stay to torture and torment, to fester, leaving behind suppurating sores that bleed.

So Dadi did the next best thing. She took me to the bathroom, put me under the shower and turned it on. Jets of water fell on my naked flesh and Dadi rubbed me vigorously with Dettol soap, as if the strong antiseptic smell would wash away all the filth, and leave me invigorated, like a child reborn. But I was not Christ resurrected—I was Jayati, soiled, debased, defiled and broken, who had been brutally raped by two men.

"I will marry her, of course," said Rajesh, who was sitting in the drawing room with his hands on his face, and Dadi heaved a sigh of relief. There was no need to go to the police. He would marry me. But that answered nothing. It would not heal me or my scars. But for Dadi, it was a reprieve. Soiled goods were being sold. With a no-return policy.

But the trauma recurred. It recurred on the wedding night itself, when I screamed, "No, no," as Rajesh came near me, and clawed his chest, my nails long and sharp, the weals red and angry. "No, no," I said, as I raised my knee and hit him in his groin.

He doubled up in pain, his face ashen, and said, "I was not even going to touch you; I was just picking up my pillow to sleep on the couch."

I was stricken when I saw his face.

He never touched me again, although on several nights I heard his low moans and the words, "Jaya, Jaya," coming gutturally from somewhere deep inside his throat. So that is what he calls me, I thought to myself, one part of me wanting to go to him and surrender and the other ready to give him a well-deserved kick if he dared to touch me.

A few days later his leave was over and he went away, while I returned to Dadi's house, like Rajesh wanted, because living in his grandmother's house without him by my side would have been daunting.

"Perhaps you should find something to keep you busy," suggested Dadi.

I bristled with anger. "After what has happened to me, you still suggest I go out to earn a living?"

"Well, you can't live all your life like a lizard hiding under a rock," she said practically.

"What do you know about what I have undergone?" I said woodenly. "You have led such a sheltered life." The next minute I wanted to bite my tongue. Dadi had faced trauma of a different kind. She had lost her husband, son and daughter-in-law, when the bus taking them to Shimla had overturned and fallen into a ravine. Thank God for the life insurance company in which Papa had worked and the hefty insurance policies he had bought in Dadaji, Mummy and his own names. At least we were left comfortably off, and I do not remember Dadi shedding tears any time during my childhood.

"My tears had dried up by then." This time it was Dadi's voice that was wooden.

"Why?" I said.

"Do you know that we came from Lahore, after crossing the border during Partition?" she asked, opening up at last.

"Oh!" I said. "I didn't know."

"Well, when I was crossing the border with my family, I got left behind. I joined them in a refugee camp four days later."

"What happened to you?" I asked her.

"Whatever happened to you," she said. Then she was silent and stone-faced.

"How many were they?" I asked, unable to restrain myself.

"I don't know," she said, in a voice so low that I had to bend my head to hear her. "I lost count. And it lasted two days."

"Why didn't you commit suicide?" I asked her with the callousness of the young.

"Because I loved life," she said, with a sudden burst of anger. "Because I wanted to live. Because this was an aberration. It was an assault on my body, but not on my mind. Because even when it was happening, I had separated my body from my mind, and not let what was happening touch my being. I wanted to live, Jayati," she said, her voice growing stronger. "Was that so wrong? I wanted to watch every sunrise and sunset. I wanted to smell the fragrance of jasmine and savour the smell of the rain-washed earth. I wanted to dance in the rain. There were so many things I wanted in life. I didn't want half a dozen or even a dozen bastards to ruin it all for me. I blanked my mind. I was a cadaver and they were all bastards desecrating the dead. The girl in me, whom they wanted to rape, was never there at all.

"I was not the only one," she added. "There were many girls like me who were casualties of Partition. Some jumped before coming trains. Some survived to live a long life. I met my family in the refugee camp three days after I had got left behind. They didn't ask me what had happened to me during those three days. I didn't tell them either. I was just glad that I was alive."

I looked at her careworn, weather-beaten face, with deep lines that often crinkled with laughter. I had always assumed they were laugh lines. Now I knew better. "How old were you when it happened, Dadi?" I was about to ask her. But I knew Dadi was born in 1935. She was 12 years old when it had happened. I was speechless. I was 22.

Maybe Dadi's stoicism rubbed off me when three months after my marriage I discovered that I was pregnant. Dadi smiled. She had no reasons at all to believe that the child was not Rajesh's.

"I will have an abortion," I told Rajesh when I rang him up to tell him.

He sounded subdued. "No, your life may be in danger. The mandatory 16 weeks are over," he said. "Now you should have the baby."

"Don't be Mother Teresa," I barked over the phone. "Our marriage will never work if we have a child who is a constant reminder of that evening."

"Do you think that not having the child will wipe away whatever happened that evening?" he asked.

Hearing him, I was reminded of his groans, "Jaya, Jaya," while tossing and turning in his sleep.

I was sure that Mother Teresa was wrong when she spoke against abortion. But then Mithun was born and I found that she was right after all. It did not matter that Rajesh was not the father; it did not matter whose Y chromosome had mixed with my X chromosome. Nothing mattered but the wonder that was Mithun.

Rajesh took leave and came back when Mithun was born. When he saw Mithun for the first time, something changed within him. The remote, reticent air surrounding him disappeared and I saw the animated happy man he must have been before he was cloaked in a shroud of guilt.

Six years later I went to Tanghdhar in Kashmir. "It is beautiful," Rajesh had written. "Although it is a non-family station, it is open to spouses for a month."

It was my first visit to Kashmir. I saw the snowcapped mountains and breathed the fresh air and felt reborn.

Perhaps I could put the past behind me. Finally. I looked at the treacherous roads with the hairpin bends, the Jhonga that took me to the barracks, the family accommodation that was available to us for just one month, and fell in love with it all.

On the last day of my trip the commanding officer threw a party to celebrate his promotion. It was the first time in my life that I had champagne.

"It is mandatory," said Rajesh, "to raise a toast and to drink champagne."

But after the three toasts made by the commanding officer, his next-in-command and someone else, the champagne hit me, the floor began to look uneven and I was afraid to pass out. Once in our own accommodation I fell on the bed, and as Rajesh bent down to pick up his pillow I pulled him down towards me, and held him tight. And Rajesh, who too had had the three mandatory toasts, struggled momentarily and said, "Jaya, Jaya, please don't!" and I giggled. In the morning I looked at him with tenderness. At last I had put the past behind me.

That was three months ago. That was the last I saw of him. Until now, at his cremation.

It takes a short time. Rajesh had wanted the electric crematorium, I am told. And now that he is no more, how can I ignore his last wishes? Mithun stands by my side. He clutches my hand and holds on to it tight. He is bewildered by what is going on. He is too young to understand the meaning of cremation, although he was a part of the ceremonies.

"God, I am hungry," I mutter once we reach home.

Dadi is shocked. She tells me that she had not eaten for a week when the news of the accident that killed Dadaji and my parents had reached her.

"I want to have paratha and mango pickle," I say.

"We cannot light a kitchen fire at home," she retorts, reminding me of an old custom. "Our friends will send us food."

"We have no friends," I argue. The ones we did have had also abandoned us when we were cocooned in our grief.

At last Dadi compromises. She takes out 200 rupees and sends our part-time maid to get two potato parathas and mango pickle.

"Make that six," I mutter. I am not only thinking of myself. I am also thinking of Dadi and Mithun. But he is sleeping on the bed, his face pinched and his body exhausted. Suddenly I hear him moan, "Papa, Papa."

Just like his father, I think, as I look at him with tenderness. Then I remember that Rajesh is not Mithun's father, at least not biologically. Maybe I will have to tell Mithun the truth one day.

"So will the government give you a job?" asks Dadi.

"Dadi!" I am shocked.

"But you need a job," she insists. "How much is Rajesh's pension? And now you will have one more mouth to feed."

I raise my eyebrows. She looks pointedly at my belly. I realise that I can no longer ignore the bouts of nausea that I should have diagnosed as morning sickness long ago. A shiver runs down my spine. A Rajesh Junior. A posthumous child. Do I want it or not? I know the answer to that one. Finally I admit it to myself. I had been head over heels in love with my husband all along. Even when I felt betrayed. Even though I felt let-down. As though a soldier had no right to let his guard down and fail in his duty of guarding citizens. Specifically me.

I am having the paratha with dollops of butter when I hear a knock on the door. Dadi opens it. A man dressed in army fatigues walks in with a brown Manila envelope and a small suitcase. Rajesh's personal possessions. He places the suitcase on the bed and leaves.

I browse through it hurriedly. Shirts, pants, uniform, underwear, socks. I bury my face in his clothes. I can smell him. I fight back the tears that threaten to flow. It is not good for the baby, I tell myself fiercely. Then I look at the wallet. It seems a little old and careworn. It contains a lot of cash. And only one photo. I slide the photo out and smile in anticipation.

But it is not mine and Mithun's. It is of a girl with large limpid eyes and long flowing tresses, a girl whose eyes seem to glow and whose smile dazzles.

Everything falls into place. Rajesh's reticence when he came to see me, his reluctance to ask me anything at home, his preoccupation with his thoughts when we were in the Buddha Jayanti Park, his stoic, "I shall marry her, of course," when he was being torn asunder by the choice he had to make, his crying, "Jaya, Jaya," in his sleep, the love he gave up because of what happened that day, the sacrifice he made when he gave up his love to salvage a woman's honour.

I read the inscription behind the photograph: "To Rajesh, with all my love, Jaya."

# Identity Crisis

The lift seems cramped, although it can take four people, or 270 kilograms in terms of weight. As of now, it can accommodate one more. A man enters the lift and presses a button, and as the lift moves upwards the atmosphere becomes electric. I look at his curly brown hair, grey-blue eyes, high cheekbones, aquiline nose and cleft chin and am shocked. He seems to be the mirror image of my son Rohit. In comparison, my husband Raghav, with his medium height, snub nose, brown eyes and thinning hair, looks like a stranger.

Rohit's eyeballs begin to protrude. If I didn't know any better I would think that they were in danger of popping out. He knows he is looking at a man who could be his double, except that he is a couple of decades older. Rohit does not believe in coincidences of this kind. Neither do I. Raghav pulls a long face. All the colour has drained from it. He looks at Rohit and then at the stranger. His eyes dart from one to the other, not knowing what to say. I stand in a corner, the eternal bystander, wondering who the man is. I do not believe in doppelgangers. I suspect neither do Raghav and Rohit.

Reactions begin to set in. Rohit digs his nails into his palms. His eyes glance at the stranger and then turn to me accusingly. He has judged me and found me guilty. He glances at Raghav pityingly. He is judgemental. Perhaps all teenagers are. He has been reading *Cuckold* by Kiran Nagarkar. It would not take a genius to figure out what he is thinking.

Raghav's face is deadpan. His eyes seem focused on the switchboard, though I have no idea what engages his attention. He has always been successful in hiding his feelings. 25 years of marriage and I still do not know my husband well. Does he also suspect me?

I am seething as well. Has Fate played a trick on us? Right now I am looking at the man who is towering above us, even above Rohit. He is oblivious to the drama around him. He is looking impatiently at his watch. It is a Tag Heuer—I know because Rohit chose an identical watch for his own birthday. He must have a board meeting to attend and may be getting late for it. He may be the CEO of a company. He gets out on the 10th floor without a backward glance at any one of us. We are too shocked to say anything to him.

The lift reaches the 30th floor. Raghav is the first to get out. Avoid unpleasantness: that has been his mantra, and he thinks that, having shut the lift door behind him, he has cut off that chapter of his life. We walk ahead, leaving a shocked and befuddled Rohit to trail behind us.

The suite Raghav has booked for us at the holiday inn is huge. The Manhattan Holiday Inn, with 50 floors, is the tallest holiday inn in the world. I had been enthralled when we had first checked in. The antechamber has a comfortable sofa that converts into a bed. An LED TV hangs on the wall. Two prints, a Monet and a Da Vinci, hang on another wall. The bedroom has a spectacular view of New York, the one city I have always wanted to visit. The skyline is enthralling. As is the sight of the serene Hudson River, which flows in the distance. I look out of the window and see the 9/11 memorial we had just visited that morning. While paying homage to those who had died, we were not aware of the drama which awaited us on our return.

New York. The city that never sleeps. I smile satirically at the irony of it. I know that we will not be able to sleep tonight and many nights after that.

Raghav sits on the couch with his head bowed. He picks up the television remote and begins to change channels. No soap opera can match our own, but Raghav seems to be oblivious of the fact. He would do anything to avoid a confrontation. And I know that is what we are heading for. But I forget. Raghav is an ostrich. Right now his head is deeply buried in the sand.

I have to take the challenge head on. "I am furious; I shall sue the clinic," I rant. "There must have been a mix-up in the sample—just how careless or unethical is that?"

"What do you think happened?" Raghav asks.

"They used the wrong sperm, or maybe they implanted the wrong sperm and ovum into me." Have I borne the child of another man unwittingly or am I merely a surrogate? Is Raghav and my child growing up in another man's home? Maybe in New York itself? Or is Rohit really my son, fathered by a stranger? I wish the man in the lift had not been so self-absorbed. I wish he had taken a good look at Rohit. Then maybe we would have had some answers. Or maybe a flurry of questions.

Rohit enters the antechamber a few minutes later. I hear him turn the key and then dump his bag on the settee on which he has been sleeping. He then bangs open our bedroom door without ceremony—an act of discourtesy he would normally never commit.

I wonder where he has been. To cry? Or to compose himself? Or did he wait outside to rehearse what he is going to say to us? Rohit anticipates fireworks. I guess as much. Does he expect accusations of infidelity to be hurled against me? Does he expect threats of divorce?

"Mom," he says, his eyes accusing, "whose son am I?" He is not prepared for my answer.

"That is what we are trying to figure out, son."

The time has come to tell him the truth—that he was not born the way billions of children are, but was conceived in a Petri dish, and then implanted back into my womb. A child born thanks to IVF, a technique barely in existence so many years ago in India. But it appears that the hospital messed it up. Was it the careless mixing of samples? I glance at Rohit and see the look of aversion in his eyes. His eyes keep darting to Raghav. But Raghav's face is expressionless. Only one thing registers with Rohit—that he was a mistake.

"I shall sue the hospital," I say, forgetting that Rohit is the child I nurtured in my womb for nine months. Forgetting that I nursed him at my breast, forgetting the nights I kept awake because of him and the adventures I had with him when I took him to the museum, the zoo, and for long walks in the parks. Everything was washed away the minute a man, 6'2", the mirror image of my son, walked into the lift, wreaking havoc with our lives.

I look up and see Raghav looking at me speculatively. The anger that I feel towards the doctor begins to be directed against Raghav. I seethe with indignation. Does Raghav suspect me of infidelity? Does he think that the sessions we had with Dr Sumedha were a charade? After all, I was always capable of conceiving a child. But I cannot say anything to Raghav, who is looking as impassive as ever.

I begin to feel guilty. I have no idea how Raghav is feeling. Is he distraught? Is he suspicious? I do not know. I look at Rohit, who seems hostile. His face looks grim. His shoulders are set. His hands are balled into fists. He seems to be itching for a showdown. "Don't look at us this way," I want to tell him, "we are not your enemies." I do not want Rohit to feel unloved. We may not be his biological parents, but people love their adopted children like their own, don't they?

Raghav gets up and begins to straighten a flower vase. He turns his back to me. The clink of the vase is irritating. As he bends his shirt comes out of his waistband. It annoys me too but I do not want to get up and tuck it in. The gesture would smack of intimacy and it seems that we have turned into strangers. Turning away from me is how he coped when he could not consummate our marriage. For years I slept on the crook of his arm, hoping that one day he would. He had tears in his eyes every time he tried, and many times when he didn't. "I am sorry." Those are the only words he said.

Our trip to the US is jinxed. I think we all realised it the moment Rohit's doppelganger entered the lift. We cannot converse normally with each other any more. We are keen to return to India.

Back at home in Delhi, my eyes shift to Raghav repeatedly. I hope he does not think that Rohit is the result of my extramarital affair with the man with grey-blue eyes. The travesty of it all makes me want to scream. For 28 years I have lived a lie with consummate skill, because I did not want to shame Raghav publicly. But I cannot take this lying down. I decide to return to the clinic to uncover the truth. Raghav cannot protest. He needs to know the truth as much as I do.

It is good that the doctor who attended to us still works in the hospital. Dr Sumedha's beady little eyes peer at me through black-rimmed glasses. "Yes?" she says questioningly, her voice stern. Raghav sits beside me, clucking his tongue. I decide to take the bull by its horns. "While in New York," I say, barely able to control my anger, "we saw a man who was the mirror image of my son."

She clears her throat and begins to speak. I cut her short. "Please do not give me any nonsense about a doppelganger, or about everyone having seven lookalikes in this world," I say. "I know all that. This man looked exactly like Rohit, but I do not know him. I had never met him before in my life. Then how come Rohit looks exactly like him? What did you do? Did you mix up the samples? What happened to our child? Or did you inject the wrong sperm into the ovum? Have I given birth to another man's child? I must know. I have the right to know. This is doing no good to our marriage."

Dr Sumedha's voice is chilling but emphatic. "There is no mistake," she says. "We do not make that kind of mistake."

I then see her give a sidelong glance to Raghav and I see his face droop. He knows that she will sacrifice him if need be. Suddenly it clicks. I understand it all. This was not a mistake. This was an elaborate charade which was carried out with Raghav's consent. Or was it at Raghav's behest? But why? And the answer comes to me.

I grab the file Dr Sumedha has before her. She shouts at me, trying to prevent me from snatching it. Raghav yelps. I flip open the page and see Raghav's report. Azoospermia. No sperm count. Raghav could not have fathered a child. Not Rohit. Nor anyone else. And he was not man enough to tell me that. So the idea of a donor sperm, without of course letting me into the secret, because he knew that I would object violently. It was one thing to live life as a celibate even though I was married. It was one thing to spend lonely days and nights tossing and turning in bed, longing for a physical relationship with my husband. It was another thing to bear the child of a stranger.

I was not that desperate to be a mother. For the past 18 years Raghav and I had bonded over Rohit's birth, even though our marriage was never consummated. But as Raghav suffered from erectile dysfunction, that was just not possible. But I had not known the truth about Rohit's birth.

I walk out of the doctor's room. "Naina, listen," shouts Raghav. But I continue to walk towards the car park, without a backward glance. We return home in silence. At home I begin to pack my bags. "Naina, listen," says Raghav. I had listened to him. I wish I hadn't. For 28 long years I had yearned for him with a growing ache. For all those years I had maintained the charade of a happy marriage because I did not want to shame him. But no more.

Rohit deserves to know the truth and then decide on what to do, although I know that he will pack his bags and go back to New York to hunt for his birth father. As for myself, it is time for me to leave, and to live my life on my own terms.

# Acknowledgements

Certain stories have been previously published and appear in this book with the permission of the publishers. The stories are the following: 'Blood Lies', 'The Atonement', 'Betrayal' and 'Death Wish' (Unisun Publications); 'Cry, My Beloved Child' (Srishti Books); 'If Only' (Fortytwo Bookz Galaxy); 'The Saviour' (*Good Housekeeping*); and 'Death' (Spider Thief Publishing).